D1455480

9 781943 885145

Join the Bluestocking League in celebrating the wonder of traditional <u>Regency romance</u>.

Unveiling Love

A London Regency Suspense Tale:
Episode IV

Vanessa Riley

Books by Vanessa Riley

Madeline's Protector

Swept Away, A Regency Fairy Tale

The Bargain, A Port Elizabeth Tale, Episodes I-IV

Unveiling Love, Episodes I-IV

Unmasked Heart, A Regency Challenge of the Soul Series

Sign up at VanessaRiley.com for contests, early releases, and more.

Copyright © 2016 Vanessa Riley

Published by BM Books

A Division of Gallium Books

Suite 236B, Atlanta, GA 30308

ISBN-13: 978-1-943885-14-5

SAVING A MARRIAGE OR WINNING THE TRIAL OF THE CENTURY

Dear Lovely Reader,

Unveiling Love is a serialized historical romance or soap opera told in episodes. Each episode averages three to eight chapters, about 18,000 to 30,000 words. Each episode resolves one issue. Emotional cliffhangers may be offered, but the plot, the action of the episode, will be complete in resolving this issue.

My promise to you is that the action will be compelling, the romance passionate, and the journey like nothing you've read before. I will tell you in the forward the length. This episode, Episode IV, is ten chapters long, 35,000 words. Enjoy this Regency Romance.

Vanessa Riley

Winning in the courts, vanquishing England's foes on the battlefield, Barrington Norton has used these winner-take-all rules to script his life, but is London's most distinguished mulatto barrister prepared to win the ultimate fight, restoring his wife's love?

Amora Norton is running out of time. The shadows in her mind, which threaten her sanity and alienate Barrington's love, have returned. How many others will die if she can't piece together her shattered memories? Can she trust that Barrington's new found care is about saving their marriage rather than winning the trial of the century?

In this episode:

Amora Norton needs to make all the victims of the Dark Walk Abductor truth-tellers, and she will risk all, her health and her heart, to see justice. She now understands she'll never have peace until everything is made known. Yet, will she survive disappointing Barrington one final time?

Barrington Norton refuses to lose one more thing and will stop Amora from risking her life to catch a killer. This barrister will take it upon himself to protect her and will sentence the monster who has stolen everything Barrington values. Nonetheless, is he willing to pay the ultimate price to make his wife whole?

Don't miss the exciting conclusion of this serial.

Sign up for my newsletter at www.vanessariley.com or www.christianregency.com. Notices of releases, contests, my Regency Lover's pack, and other goodies will be made available to you.

Dedication

I dedicate this book to my copy editor supreme, my mother, Louise, my loving hubby, Frank, and my daughter, Ellen. Their patience and support have meant the world to me.

I also dedicate this labor of love to critique partners extraordinaire: June, Mildred, Lori, Connie, and Gail.

Love to my mentor, Laurie Alice, for answering all my endless questions.

Love to Sharon & Kathy, they made me feel the emotion. You're never second place in my heart.

And I am grateful for my team of encouragers: Sandra, Michela, Felicia, Piper, and Rhonda.

CAST OF PRIMARY CHARACTERS

Barrington Norton: a barrister by trade, he is a free-borne mulatto gentleman of a wealthy black merchant's daughter and a landowner's ne'er-do-well son.

Amora Norton: the wife of Barrington Norton. She is of mixed blood, the daughter of an Egyptian woman and a wealthy Spanish apple merchant.

Henutsen Tomàs: Amora's Egyptian mother.

Smith: a man convicted of coining.

Cynthia Miller: a songstress and sister of Gerald Miller.

Gerald Miller: Barrington's best friend who saved his life during the Peninsula War.

Mr. Beakes: Barrington's solicitor.

Vicar Wilson: a minister serving at St. George.

Duke and Duchess of Cheshire: the newly married interracial couple William St. Landon and Gaia Telfair, reformers.

Mrs. Gretling: an abigail to Amora.

James: a man-of-all-work to Barrington.

Mr. Charleton: a rival of Barrington from their youth.

Mr. Hessing: Barrington's mentor and barrister colleague.

Hudson Solemn: Barrington's cousin.

Chapter One: Going to Bedlam

Amora took Barrington's hand and allowed his strong arms to help her down from his carriage. Her gaze fell upon the stone walls surrounding Bedlam. It took a week for Barrington and Samuel to coerce Mr. Calloway's permission. A whole seven days of trying to find things to paint, of pretending not to notice Barrington's goings and comings from the attic, or his wincing as his wound was dressed.

None of this distracted her. Only the hope of seeing Sarah kept her wits level.

James doffed his hat to her and bounced back to his post atop the carriage. "Happy hunting, sir and madam."

His man's soulful eyes bespoke his heart. He must be concerned about his master returning to Bedlam.

James leaned his head down. His gaze locked onto Barrington's. "I'll be ready to leave at a moment's notice."

Her husband nodded. "Thank you."

Barrington took her hand and led her through the courtyard. His posture hunched as if weighted by all the heaviness of the world. Perhaps his hip still bothered him. A week from being nearly beaten to death wasn't enough time to heal.

She stopped, reached up and adjusted his cravat, fluffing the folds of the bright white lawn fabric. "This will go well."

He clasped her hand and looked down upon her. His silvery gray eyes seemed so distant. No crinkles formed of humor, just harsh lines from lack of sleep, or worse, fear. "It's not too late." His tone was low. It bordered upon desperate. "We can get an ice. Do anything else, but this."

Fingers intertwined, he pressed closer, folding her within his iron embrace. His lips slipped to her brow. "We could leave London forever. We could travel. We could see the world. Let me give you the world, Amora."

He'd only begged once in his life that she'd witnessed and that was the day she tried to toss herself off the cliff in Clanville.

Was that it?

Did he assume she'd lose her reason knowing the truth? Couldn't he see it was the only way to keep her wits? She brought her dark indigo gloved hands to his chin. "The truth will set us free. Trust in me, please."

His gray eyes darted. His lips pressed into a firmer line. Surely, he couldn't pledge to completely trust in her. It wasn't in him to lie.

But she had faith in herself. It might be small and mangled, but it was hers. She could no longer rest without knowing, not anymore. Only the truth could save her.

They plodded up the stairs. Barrington held open the door and allowed her inside. The stench of mustard and tonics wafted down the corridor. She put a hand to her nose. The place was dark.

Barrington tugged his hat off. He trudged back and forth waiting. "Mr. Greene, the caregiver, will be here soon."

He stopped by a door and touched the handle. "To think, Miller was here all that time. I could've visited him if Miss Miller had been honest."

"Those words don't seem to go together, Miss Miller and honesty."

A tall grim-faced man cleaning his large onyx spectacles appeared at the entrance of the long hall.

Barrington walked over to him and shook his hand. "I'm Barrister Norton. You're Mr. Greene?"

"That I am." He tweaked his thick mustache. "The head administrator of Bethlehem Hospital. I understand you want to see Miss Calloway. It's getting a bit late in the evening for visiting."

Barrington nodded. His fingers fumbled along the brim of his top hat. "Miss Calloway is a potential witness to a crime. She's one of the Dark Walk Abductor's victims."

"Crying shame what they say happened."

Like awakening from a fog, Barrington stepped forward. His grip tightened on his hat, almost as if thumbs would pierce the fabric. "It did happen. We just don't know who the villain is."

"Well, let's see if the woman is not so dour tonight." Waving, Mr. Greene led them down a long hall. "Miss Calloway disappeared from Vaux Hall and was found a month later, babbling in a ditch a few hours outside of London. Horrible condition."

A few hours? Amora thought. That could be Clanville,

couldn't it? If this woman was Sarah, then Barrington was right. Amora swallowed. How much would her world change knowing that the Dark Walk Abductor held her captive?

Voices echoed.

Unintelligible mumblings seemed to crowd them as they paced deeper into the building. A darkened room of beds and bodies lay to the right.

Greene trudged past, head held high as if the patients were part of the wall. How could one grow cold to human misery?

The administrator's snow covered head stopped bobbing in front of an illuminated entry. It stood apart in the dim passageway, the only door with light pouring from the frame.

Barrington's countenance dimmed. "She needs a great deal of light even in the evenings when she should be sleeping?"

Greene huffed, as if the burden to not be overtaken by darkness was something one could help. "Miss Calloway is quiet if we keep her room lit." He pulled out a skeleton key from his long coat and pressed it into the lock.

As Amora followed, the smells of urine and stale air assaulted her. The familiar toxic perfume wrenched at her soul. Oh, how she'd rather smell the stinging scent of lye soap from the asylum or even wretched chrysanthemums. Her fingers trembled. She stuffed her hands into her pockets.

A lump with blonde hair rolled into a ball was chained to the bed.

Two makeshift wall sconces were attached to the plain gray wall. Large candles burned from them. If the candles were snuffed, the poor girl and everyone in the room wouldn't see more than a few inches forward. Amora's heart raced. Being trapped in this small space with no light would be death.

Almost as if her mind had willed it, one of the wicks lost its flame. The dimmed light of the space raced her pulse, but fear wouldn't stop her from knowing the truth.

"Fool light. Would be the way when I come for this one." Mr. Green shook his head then palmed the wall, knocking as if to rouse a mute. "Miss Calloway, you have visitors."

The woman shivered and tugged on her stained brown blanket. The thick metal links chimed, clinking with each movement.

"Do you..." Barrington's eyes darted. He fanned his nose. "Do you have to keep them like this?"

"We're shorthanded and ill-funded. We get a little over three shillings a week per lunatic. Her family pays a little more so she's not in the open room with the rest."

Wrenching his neck, Barrington shook his head. "That's barely a bag of sugar. Certainly not enough for a proper diet and care. If someone were kept on an upper floor, how much would that be?"

Mr. Greene poked at the woman. "More."

"We've come on short notice. Do you at least clean her up for visits with her family?" Barrington's strong voice bellowed, echoing in the small room. "They shouldn't see her like this."

Painful laughter dripped from the administrator's lips. "No one visits her. The Calloways have three other daughters to wed. They consider this one deceased to not detract from the others' chances." The smirk on his face erased. "Does anyone have enough time to deal with the unfortunate?"

Barrington's face dipped. He gazed toward the floor as if it held one of his law books. "We need to make time. Love and decency demands it."

Amora heard regret echo in Barrington's low tone. Her heart trembled. She had regrets, too. Barrington had placed himself in jeopardy taking her to Bedlam, the place where he'd pilfered Miller. If anything untoward happened to her husband, those regrets would burn her up inside. She mouthed, "I'm sorry," but he never looked up, never saw how her heart had turned toward him again.

Heavier and harder, Mr. Greene pounded the wall once more. The rhythmic tap, tap, tap sounded like falling bricks. "Wake up, Miss Calloway."

He turned his hardened grimace toward Barrington. "Better here where we can keep the poor girl from mischief or suicide."

Beneath Amora's palm, the muscles in Barrington's arms tensed. "Greene, stop. The lady does not seem to want to speak with us." He raised head and caught Amora's gaze. "Come along, my dear."

No, she couldn't. Not with so many questions. With a pat to his forearm, Amora left his side. She inched toward the bed until she stood directly underneath the precious candle. "Miss Calloway. Can you hear me?"

No response came from the poor woman, but Amora had come too far to be deterred. She needed to touch the woman, to see if she was her Sarah. Amora's soul felt cut in two. She wanted her Sarah. But if this woman was she, then that would mean Barrington was right. The Dark Walk Abductor was her monster.

Mr. Greene stepped between Amora and the inmate's bed. "Miss Calloway, visitors have come to see you."

"Has he come to make it dark again?" A feeble voice emanated from the pile of curly blond hair. "Will you torment me again?"

"No, ma'am." Mr. Greene stepped away. "She's not going to cooperate. I've got another appointment."

Amora slipped past him and put her hand on Sarah's head. "Let us stay with her a few minutes. You can go about your day."

"Fine." The administrator headed to the door. She's chained so I don't think she could escape from here."

He eyed Barrington before he exited and closed the door behind him.

Her husband left his perch from the wall and came to her. He gripped Amora's shoulder. "We shouldn't stay. I have a bad feeling."

She glanced at him and saw fear in the wide irises of his eyes. Was it fear of being discovered for Miller's extrication or fear that Amora would become like this Sarah?

"That grace in the song you taught me, maybe it's enough to keep me from here."

"His grace is sufficient. Through toils and strife, Amora. It's sufficient, beyond strife in marriage, through turmoil like this."

She nodded. For the first time in a long time, that mystery called grace did feel thick and encompassing, almost healing. Almost. "Miss Calloway, lift your head. I need to see if you are my friend."

The woman pushed deeper into her blanket away from them. "No one wants to be my friend."

Amora reached for her again, this time taking off her gloves and fingering the woman's knotted locks. "Sarah, please. Show me your face. I was trapped like you. I need to know if we were trapped together."

Trembling, Miss Calloway unfurled herself. Her brown eyes, large and vacant, mirrored the candle's flame shining from the lone wall sconce.

Amora sat beside her and stared. Time had not been good to this woman. Amora's Sarah was the same age as she when they were thrust into bondage. The gold of *this* Sarah's hair had silvered.

The haggard creature looked more than ten years older. Was this her friend? She couldn't tell. A tear slipped from Amora's eye. She'd failed at pretending to be strong. No, that grace wasn't resilient. "I don't know if she's my Sarah, Barr. I don't know anything."

He opened his arms wide. "You know enough. Come to me, brave girl."

Before Amora could move from the bed and toss herself into Barrington's safe embrace, the woman reached out with a dirty palm and caught Amora's cheek.

"It's me. Sarah. Know me, even if I can't remember you."

"Sweetheart, move from her."

Barrington's hushed tone caught Amora's attention as did his warning, but Sarah's bony fingers had looped into her bonnet strings. Fear didn't squeeze at Amora's heart, but the anxiety of never knowing the truth did. She brushed the hair from Sarah's temples exposing healed scars. "Is it you? Were we together in the Priory, the old ruins? In my dreams, I hear the bricks falling every night. Do you?"

Chains clinked and clanged as the chained woman knocked the bonnet off Amora's head and pressed ragged nails into Amora's chin. Sarah said, "His pet, did you come *for her*? I hear you moaning, panting for light. Is he coming? Did he send you?"

"Mrs. Norton." Barrington pulled Amora from the bed. "Miss Calloway's too far gone. Let's get you out of here."

Clang, Clang. Sarah pulled on her chains as if to break free from the bed. "Don't leave me. No more darkness. Don't hurt me because I'm not her. I'll do anything. Consent. I consent." She yanked her blanket from her legs. "Consent."

Barrington threw the wool back onto her limbs. "So, the tales of depravity are true. The Dark Walk Abductor made you harlot yourself for freedom. What did this man look like?"

Miss Calloway's eyes grew wide. "The man in the dark."

Barrington stooped near. "The man in the dark, was his arms skinny or thick?"

"Thick like a tree trunk." She pried her fingers apart as if they straddled a huge log. Her chewed nails wiggled over an imagined circumference of at least sixteen inches. "He threw me against a curved wall. Slammed my head. His heavy weight smothered everything. Nothing but night." She dropped her face into her knees.

"Poor creature." Barrington stood and towed Amora to him, his hands cupping her abdomen. "Providence kept my mind safe through four long years of war. He's helped you with your battles. God should be able to restore this girl."

"Hypocrite." Sarah's voice sounded loud, strident. "We prayed to God, but He didn't help. Did He, Amora?" The lass wept and slumped back into a ball. "Only helps those not trapped in the ruins."

"She said my name! Barrington, she called to me." She pulled from him and ran to Sarah. "You do remember me. You remember the ruins, the Priory." She wrapped the frail woman into her arms.

Tears flowed from Amora, pouring out of every reserve and hidden place inside. Someone else could attest to what happened. Sarah wasn't a figment of her imagination. They were together, and they both lived.

Yet, that meant the worse was also true.

Sarah was a Dark Walk Abductor victim.

Then, Amora must be too.

Amora couldn't breathe. She opened her mouth, hoping to suck in air, but nothing came in or out. Not until Barrington gripped her hand and kissed the bulging veins of her wrist.

He stooped again, perhaps he knelt. "Miss, God does help and He hasn't forgotten you or your plight." His gaze locked with Amora's. "Some of God's miracles take longer."

Sarah shook head, her eyes slimming to slits. "But you will forget me."

Amora wiped her face against the sleeve of her spencer. "I won't. I've been desperate to remember you, to see you in places other than my nightmares."

"He's coming. Hear his footsteps?" Sarah started to shriek and yanked at clumps of her hair.

Barrington stepped near the door. "We should leave Miss Calloway in peace."

"He's coming! He's coming for her, for her." She started hitting herself with the chain links.

Amora covered Sarah up, holding her arms so she couldn't hurt herself. "The monster's gone from here."

The administrator opened the door, "Boy, boy, come

here. I need help."

The man trailed back into the hall. "Boy!"

Barrington stood, his honey-colored complexion seemed to pale. Could the lad identify him?

Her wonderful husband caught her gaze, and puffed out his chest with pride. "I am prepared for anything."

Her husband couldn't end up in Newgate prison.

Panic at losing him pinched at her side. A dull ache, familiar and strong, pinched at her middle. She lifted her head to peer over Sarah, spying the candle.

She patted her mumbling friend, then popped up close to the candle and reached for the wick.

"Don't, Amora. I have to face my actions." Before Barrington could stop her, she took a breath and snuffed the light.

Darkness fell upon her, just like in the Priory, in her cell. Amora's pulse pounded. She doubled over as the pain increased. A scream broke from her mouth.

"Amora! Where are you, Amora?"

She moved from the deep voice. It was a trick. Barr was at war, not trapped with the monster.

The feel of someone's breath on her neck set every nerve on fire.

The sound of dragging footsteps forced her to her knees. Amora screamed at things touching her. No man could have her. She hit the unmovable arms, the bands of iron coming at her. She yelled for no one but God, for no person ever came. No one.

Still, she fought. Her no's blended with Sarah's.

The music of Sarah's voice guided Amora to her friend.

Just like before, she took Sarah's hand and threaded her arms about her. "Together, we fight."

Sarah stopped shrieking and held onto her. "Together."

Once again, it was them against the beast.

Amora closed her eyes and let the pitch dark hide them.

Barrington hunted his pockets, desperate for his lighter. It popped out and slid into the darkness of the floor. Useless.

His attempts to grab Amora ended with a punch to his cheek. She needed to see his face to know it was him and not her abductor. "Amora, it's me. Barrington. I'll get you light. Hold on for the light."

Feeling his way back to the entrance in the now silent room, everything within him cringed and twisted.

He reached for the door, but his head bounced as it flung open sending him crashing into the wall. A man blocked the hall light, keeping it from his terrified wife and her Sarah. "What the devil is going on in here?"

"Sir, what did you want?"

Another voice. Could it be the young man who led Barrington to Miller? Barrington came from behind the door and held up his wrists to be led away to the magistrate. Then, he realized the darkness hid his hands, too. Amora had sacrificed herself for him again. Just as she did when the cliff gave way, and the night Beakes came to Mayfair.

"Excuse me, sir." Greene knocked into Barrington as he pushed inside. "Boy! Go get a lantern and a doctor from upstairs."

"Yes, sir." The pounding of the lad's boots faded.

Amora had saved Barrington. What a woman!

But, at what cost? His heart thundered anew.

With only the sound of Greene's fussing and stomping, the room was eerily quiet. "Miss Calloway, look at the light from the hall."

"Yes, Amora. You look too. It's not dark outside this room. Let's leave."

"No one move," Greene said. "I don't want Miss Calloway more agitated. She could be a danger to herself."

When it came to his wife, Barrington would wait for no one. His angel was in the grips of an insane woman, covered in mind-numbing terror. What if Miss Calloway strangled his love? With no answer, he elbowed past Greene. "Amora?"

Barrington trudged over to the wall and fingered it until he found the sconce. From an inner pocket in his greatcoat, he located some flint. It would have to do. With a prayer and groan, it lit the candle.

Like a soft whisper in the woods, the light grew and spread, filling the room. When he turned to the bed, his heart flung past his hurting ribs and jammed into his throat.

Amora had fainted and lay atop the cot, huddled back to back arms interlocked at the elbows with Miss Calloway. Each woman faced a different direction. A protective stance, probably meant to keep them safe from an approaching assault.

Everything hurt all over again.

He neared the women, untwisted their limbs, and pulled his wife from the bed tucking her safely into his arms. "I have you, Mrs. Norton. I'm never letting go. We're leaving, Mr. Greene."

"Your wife...she knows Miss Calloway. She's a victim, too."

"Don't. Don't leave me, Amora." Sarah sat up. "They don't understand."

Amora roused with wide blinking eyes. "She's real, Barrington."

She felt so weak in his arms. Her listless mouth mumbled, "I didn't lie,"

With flailing arms, Miss Calloway reached for her. "Please, don't go."

But nothing would take Amora from him, not now, not ever. "I have to take my wife home, but we won't forget you. We'll visit again. You've been…" He cleared his parched throat. "Most helpful."

Greene caught Barrington's arm, stopping his retreat. "Can you really decipher such gibberish?"

He shook free, but did so without upsetting Amora. "I can. Miss Calloway's description eliminates a number of suspects. No man who has ever been less than a sack of cannonballs, maybe a hundred and thirty pounds, could be their abductor."

"That's half of London." Greene sighed and rubbed his neck. "But, no one will believe Miss Calloway. Maybe this young woman, your wife –"

"Good day, sir." Barrington stormed down the hall and out of Bedlam's doors. Amora had experienced enough, suffered too much to be on the witness box, even if it meant convicting the Dark Walk Abductor.

"Sarah lives." Amora's voice was airy as if caught in sleep. Was she in shock?

"Augh." She groaned.

The knot in Barrington's throat returned. Heaviness filled his already low spirits.

He kissed her brow. "I'm going to take you home and make you feel as safe as possible."

Across the yard and through the gates, he ran to his carriage. Cradling her as if she were a Wedgewood vase, Barrington lifted her onto the seat. Holding her hand, he knelt at her side.

Her face was more pale than before. She was in pain.

James poked his head inside the opening. "Sir, is she well? Should I fetch a doctor?"

"Let's get her home to familiar surroundings." He loosened her coat, then brushed a wayward lock that had descended from her bun.

His man nodded and shut the door.

Amora's breathing was ragged and slow.

Swallowing his fear for her life, her sanity, he put his finger to her trembling abdomen. He felt a jolt of a contraction. He hoped it was nerves. His fear of losing her and now the babe was coming to fruition.

No.

Everything in his spirit shouted it again until the word fell from his lips. "No!"

She wasn't going to lose anything else. He put both hands on her stomach. "This is your father. Stay in there. Stay well in there. It's not time. We haven't prepared for you."

Her stomach trembled again.

When would children ever listen? Maybe this one would live to be as stubborn as his mother. *Lord, help me keep them safe.*

Chapter Two: A Raid

Barrington's landau turned onto Mayfair Lane. He rocked a barely alert Amora in his arms. "We are almost home."

She was distant. With each vibration of the carriage, she bit her lip. "I'm sorry, Barr."

"For what? We found Sarah. That should make you happy."

She looped her fingers with his and pressed her stomach. "For this miscar--"

He couldn't let her say the ugly word. Then it would be true and Amora's sacrifice for his sorry hide would be complete. *Lord, please don't let it come to pass. Not again.*

His fingertips felt another smaller contraction. The babe couldn't come now, not with barely five months of stewing. But hadn't he known this would happen?

She closed her eyes again. "Proof... not a liar."

What delusion made him think it was a good idea to take her to Bedlam to see Sarah Calloway? He should've gone with his gut, not that desperate look in her eyes.

Yet, Amora had become like himself needing to claim

her own proof. Now this quest could cost everything.

If they lost this child, Amora might slip into a depression or worse, lose her reason like the other victims.

And how would he get along, knowing he allowed all of this to happen? He should've convinced her to abandon the hunt. She didn't need any more proof. She needed to accept she was a Dark Walk Abductor victim. "Lord, let her come back to herself, in her right mind. Don't let the monster win."

His shoulders sagged. His head dipped against the seat. She was beautiful and brave and foolhardy to thrust herself into darkness for him. He should rot in Newgate for all the hurt he'd caused.

He brushed a curly tendril from her forehead, then traced an eyebrow. "You may not be able to hear me, you may not even feel the same, but know I love you, Amora." *God of Heaven, save my family.*

The landau stopped in front of their town home behind two other carriages. Who visited Mayfair? His stomach knotted tighter. These didn't appear to be delivery wagons.

Opening the door of the carriage, James tilted his head to the foreign carriages. "Sir, are you sure you and the misses want to return home?"

"My wife needs to rest in her own bed, whether I'm in Newgate or not. Go get my cousin."

"Yes, sir."

He eased off the seat and hoisted Amora into his arms. He'd get her settled with her mother then face the penalties of stealing Miller. If runners were scouring his house, maybe they'd let Barrington stay with his wife until the worst was over. The temptation to pull his pistol from beneath the seat pressed, but he'd use his words not bullets to keep his family.

Amora shifted her head against his shoulder. "Love you, too."

He closed his eyes for a second as he reached the door. When was the last time she'd said that to him? The night they conceived this miracle she spoke of guarding their love, but not of loving him.

But his feelings for her were so much more, had always been that way since the moment he spied her painting in Tomàs Orchards. He pressed her slim body against his heart. "I love you so much it hurts."

After a few raps with his elbow, Mrs. Gretling opened the door. Her skin was flush. "Mr. Norton, the house is in chaos." Her light eyes grew larger. "The mistress is unwell?"

He didn't know the answer and pressed inside. "Get Mrs. Tomàs. She can help." He laid Amora on the sofa in the parlor, stooped beside her and clasped her hand. "Hurry."

"Mrs. Tomàs thought ye attic project needed something extra. I believe she went to Cheapside. Then she's going to shoot her flintlock at an old friend's estate in the afternoon. Women and guns, indeed. I don't--"

There was no time for the abigail's ramblings. Frustrated, he waved a palm in the air. "What is occurring at Mayfair?"

"The workmen had just finished the painting up there in the attic. Then ye Mr. Beakes arrived and begun searching the house. Says there is a fugitive here."

Gerald. They came for his friend. How did he know Miller was here?

Barrington gazed at Amora. She laid so still. She was

everything he ever wanted. This was his fault, leaving her for the war, bringing Miller here. "James went for a doctor. Go find Mrs. Tomàs at once. Tell her Amora's having contractions."

"She's birthing? What? Are you sure? It's too soon. Not another baby lost." Mrs. Gretling covered her mouth and ran from the room.

Maybe the Pharaoh had a witches' brew that could do some good. Barrington was just about desperate for anything. He turned and spied his mother-in-law's idols on the mantle. Well, almost anything. He hadn't lost his mind to grief...yet.

Whipping off his coat, he bundled it about Amora. Maybe he could convince his solicitor to let him stay with Amora until she and the babe were well. He'd fight with his fists to do so. Perhaps he should've brought in the pistol. One of Beake's men might attempt to stab him.

Barrington heard the pounding of boots. The men must be coming up from the basement.

He stood up straight, but laced his fingers with Amora's. "Hear me, Amora. I'm here until they drag me away."

Beakes marched into the parlor first. The drumming of his footfalls slowed and echoed on the floor, just like Barrington's heart. Anxious over Amora, Miller, and Newgate, the poor organ beat a crazed rhythm. It had surely flopped out his shirt and awaited crushing. What to do?

More boots sounded.

Barrington couldn't help but close his fingers tighter about Amora's.

"Barr, what's happening?"

He couldn't answer. Her frail voice sliced through him as a vision of poor confused Miller being dragged away filled his head. Barrington held his breath as he readied for Beakes's goons to try and move him. If he couldn't withstand them, how would Amora make it with him tossed into Newgate?

Two burly runners appeared at the threshold, without Miller.

Surprised, relieved, but not stupid, Barrington puffed out his chest covering up his complicity. He needed to act as an innocent man would to stay with Amora. "What is the meaning of this, Beakes? Why are you upsetting my household?"

"We were told the fugitive, Gerald Miller, was being aided here."

Shaking on the inside, Barrington pivoted from his solicitor and drew a handkerchief from his pocket and mopped Amora's sweating brow. "Did you find him?"

"No. But that doesn't mean he wasn't here. Someone's been living in your basement."

He placed a palm on his wife's abdomen. The quivering of stomach continued. His chest constricted more with each pulse. *Lord, where are you?* Barrington cleared his throat. "Those are servant's quarters. We have servants. Beakes, sending your mongrels at me is one thing, but to desecrate my home is another. My wife is ill. I need you to leave."

"I haven't sent anyone after you. But, I had to look. Miss Miller said the fugitive was here."

Cynthia turned in her own brother? Barrington shook his head, but his gaze stayed on Amora counting her breaths. "Why would she send you here?"

"At Hessing's insistence, I took her to the magistrate

for hiding a murderer. A night in Newgate loosened her tongue." He thumbed his jacket. "But a forked tongue. Sorry, Norton. She's probably just angered over a recent incident." He waggled a brow.

Barrington rubbed his skull. Being known as an adulterer apparently had a benefit. Surely, his wayward father must be looking up and smiling. "Newgate? That's for hardened criminals. For men."

"Hessing made sure she was safe, but he wants the Dark Walk Abductor. He'll do what he must to win."

The ominous warning foretold where Barrington now stood with his mentor. The man won at all costs and his prize project, the mulatto barrister was a liability.

Barrington heaved a tight breath. "So will you, Beakes. I received your message with the pipe to my skull." He patted his ribs. "He left a beauty stabbing me here." He released Amora's fingers and stepped to Beakes, so close the man couldn't miss a jot of Barrington's meaning. "I can take anything you can bring, but not in my house, not near my wife. Get out."

His solicitor nodded to his two grunt-like associates. They exited the parlor. "Norton, I didn't send anyone to attack you, but dealing with the Dark Walk Abductor can get you killed. I'm about the law. We all want justice."

He scanned Beakes's countenance. The smooth smirk, the rigid set of his jaw were all normal looks for him. If he didn't send the message, *For Her*, who did? Barrington shook his head, anger pulsed in his veins. "The law is personal to me. See yourself out."

Beakes frowned and then marched to the front door. "I'll keep looking for Mr. Miller. If he crosses your path, send him to the magistrate. I'd hate to darken your portico again and drag you off to Newgate, too."

As soon as the skunk was on the other side of the threshold, Barrington dropped to the floor. He slumped against the sofa, placed a palm on Amora's stomach and prayed. They were no longer trapped by lies any more. Everything was in the open. God had to be with them now. He had to be.

Amora's fingertips swept across his temples. "Go find Mr. Miller. He needs you, too."

Nothing in his life meant more than being at his wife's side. What if this shock took a deeper toll? "Miller will keep or I'll find and save him later. I'm not leaving you."

Her violet eyes dimmed. "You have to think of how to clear his name. He needs you."

"Amora, don't you want me with you?"

"He could be hurt. You can send for a doctor for me, for both of us when you find him."

Not believing her brave talk, he pressed her hand to his mouth. "You hate doctors."

"I'll be fine."

She'd rather have doctors about her than him? He took off his spectacles. "Well, I won't be fine, Amora." His soul ached. But he wasn't leaving, even if she wanted him to. "You're in my thoughts, my blood. And if you shed ours tonight, I'll be with you."

With a slow ragged breath, Amora lifted a hand to him. It fell upon his lapel. "But Mr. Miller's in trouble. Cynthia's jailed. I know how it pains you. I understand, it's like my finding Sarah. I finally understand what drives your spirit."

He scooped Amora into his arms and headed for the steps. "I'm putting you to bed. I'll go nowhere until I know all is well."

Her voice was low and soft. "Sure?"

His boot met the first tread and then the next. "You come first."

Kicking open her door, he navigated to the bed. Layer after layer - her jacket, her tucker - he stripped her until she wore nothing but a chemise. One, two. First one boot, then his other went flying. "May I sit next to you, or will that make you hurt, Amora?"

Her eyes opened. She held a weak palm to his chest. "I'm in pain if you're not here beside me when I awake."

A tremor set in his cheek. It was the fever talking, but it melted his heart. He laid next to her, coddling her until she stopped trembling.

The heat from the fireplace in her brightly lit bedroom brought moisture to Amora's brow. Hours, maybe a day had passed since her husband brought her home. She squinted at the people gathered in her room, Mama, Barrington and his cousin. All must've come to Mayfair, her bed chambers to help.

She should take another sip of the strong tea Mama had made. The chamomile and herbs tasted bitter, but soothed the rawness in her throat. "May I have some more?"

Barrington lifted the cup to her lips. Attentive and sweet, he sat on the bed. His glasses were skewed. He pushed at his rolled up shirt sleeves, moving the wrinkled linen to his elbows as if that would make it better. "Would you like something to eat?"

Mama lifted from her chair and stroked Amora's temples. "I could get some broth and crusty bread."

She pushed at the cup. Barrington lowered it to the bed table.

"I'm not hungry, but I am feeling better." Physically that was true, but right now her heart raced. Was the baby well? As if caught in slow motion, she moved her fingers from the blanket's edge, past the lace of her chemise stopping upon her abdomen. It felt full. The sheets and mattress were clean.

Barrington's warm palm covered hers. "You didn't miscarry."

Mr. Solemn, Barrington's cousin, stood in the door. "No, not this time. I suggest whatever you two were doing before this occurred to stop."

The man had a humor similar to Barrington's, but she couldn't laugh. She was too busy staring at her husband. A smile lifted her lips. "You stayed."

Mama picked up her balls of yarn. "The booties will take a while to complete. You need to keep that grandbaby safe. Lucky for us, Mr. Solemn knows herbs as well as me. They helped." She tugged at the Mechlin lace shawl draping her shoulders and headed for the door. "Mr. Norton, do a better job keeping my girl safe. You promised me and her late father."

He dipped his head and nodded.

"Well, cousin, Mrs. Norton. I'll go downstairs for a few. I'll wait for you, cousin."

Mama nodded as she and Mr. Solemn left the room.

Amora lifted Barrington's chin. "You are doing a fine job, but you know you can't always protect me. Now, please tell me we found Sarah. Let me not have dreamed it."

Barrington stood up and paced. His countenance bore a cross between confusion and anger. "We found her. You didn't dream it. Nor was it a dream. You were reckless. You could've been hurt. Miss Calloway is…"

"Say it, Barr. She's insane, crazed because of what the Dark Walk Abductor did."

"Yes." He stopped and clutched the top of the canopy. "She could've hurt you, could've strangled you in the dark."

"I needed to help you."

"How does it help me if you are hurt?" He folded his arms behind his back and started pacing again. "Let's examine the things you've done to help me. One, you omitted telling me about your abduction. Two, you fall off a cliff saving me from falling. Three, you prance around nearly naked in front of Beakes to keep me from Newgate."

"Yes, keep adding up the points against me, Barrister."

For a moment, his lips curled up. "Actually, the prancing is a point in your favor. I rather like that one, but I'm not done. Four, you shrouded yourself in darkness, placing yourself in the arms of a mad woman —all to keep my hide from Newgate. I belong in Newgate or Bedlam, if it means you would be safe and well."

She tried to rise, but the tiredness in her limbs was too great. Instead, she rolled to her side and looked at the velvet box of notes. "Could you write down that we found Sarah for me?"

"Are you listening to me, Amora?"

She fingered the nape of the box. "I'm well. You heard Mama and your cousin."

His footfalls sounded closer. When she glanced up, he hovered over her tucking and re-tucking the blankets about her. "Did you hear the part about stopping?"

"I have to know what happened to me. We can stop the monster."

He undid his horribly mangled cravat. It dripped down his neck as he opened his shirt. "We know enough. You were abducted and held captive by the Dark Walk Abductor."

"I want to remember if I saw his face. Then you could convict him."

The groan leaving him vibrated in his chest. "I am not finished with my statement, Lady Justice."

He sat on the bed and eased her head onto his lap. "We also know Gerald Miller attempted to rescue you and the other captive, Miss Druby. Both met your abductor's wrath. Gerald was pummeled senseless. Miss Druby's life was taken. You and Sarah and others were locked away in the Priory's cellars until..."

His voice diminished to nothing. He stroked her forehead. The feather light sensation and his clean bergamot smell should have calmed the growing fear pitting in her stomach. "Until what?"

He gathered her in his arms, spun her toward him so she could see his face. "Until consenting to his rape. That is why he released Miss Calloway. It had to be why he released you."

Everything ached all at once. How could Barrington believe she'd consent? "Never."

She beat at Barrington's arms, at his chest, but he held her fast.

"Hit at me. Take the evil out on me, but don't lose your reason like the others."

Tears welled in her eyes, though she clung to Barrington. "It's not true. If we went to the Priory, we could figure out how I escaped. It couldn't have been by--."

"We don't have to see it."

No. She couldn't accept it. Thinking of the monster touching her, taking away her dignity, her promise to the man she loved. "We should go to the Priory and walk those grounds. If I see it, smell it, all my memories would return."

He kissed her brow. "No."

"But it's been so wonderful working together. It's meant the world to investigate with you."

"Finding Sarah Calloway almost cost our babe, Amora. We can't risk your health, not anymore."

It took all her strength to pull away from his safety. He couldn't see her as weak. Not now. "We can go at the brightest part of the day. We can..."

"No." He ran a hand over his hair pushing the low curls into place. "The man came at each of you in the dark. I doubt any memory will illuminate his face. And if it did, you could lose your wits like the rest. You don't want the memory of it. And I don't want to share our bed with him."

A shiver raced her skin. How could he accept this?

He took one of her hands and held it, his thumb rubbed the soft space between her knuckles. "All of his victims were abused by an act meant to show love. Why must you remember that?"

She gripped the lace of her collar, bunching it about her neck. "You think I gave my consent to him?"

"None of the women were released until they consented to his rape. If Miller didn't get the chains off of your door, the blackguard did."

Air leaked from her lungs. The thudding of her heart within her ear deafened. She couldn't have let the monster have her. Were the screams in her nightmares her own? "Where is Mr. Miller? He could tell you what happened."

"I don't know where he is. And I doubt that he would disagree with my conclusion. Remember, the Dark Walk Abductor had already attacked him and killed Miss Druby before coming for you."

No, the monster couldn't have claim to any of her. She'd resisted him every day. "No, Barr. It can't be."

Barrington shifted and tugged her into his arms again. "The mind does things to protect us. You must be protected and treasured."

"I didn't consent. I couldn't have." She pounded her fists against his chest, then melted into him. She couldn't fight his logic or his strength. "I never said yes."

"Sweetheart, I know. Consent under duress is not true consent." His nostrils flared as his voice became low. "I don't think your monster asked. I think he took what he wanted."

She reared back. Could it be true?

Barrington massaged her neck. His fingers tried to ease the tension in her muscles, but she didn't want to be touched. She shrank away.

Her husband stood up causing the mattress to shake. He paced as he did in the Old Bailey when he made an argument. "Enraged over Miss Druby's attempt at escaping, the Dark Walk Abductor took his wrath out on them, flattening Miller's skull, strangling the life from her. Then he turned to you, and took what he wanted."

She absorbed his words like kerosene or whale oil on a flame. "I want him to pay. I have to remember to make him pay."

Barrington wiped at his mouth but the grim lines remained unchanged. "Don't remember anymore. Let me be the only one holding you in your memories."

"I have to know. You've never settled for half the story. Papa and I watched one of your early trials. You were relentless in seeking the truth."

"That was before the war. I was brash and young." He reached out and wrapped a lock of her hair about his pinkie. "You were too. If a life was in jeopardy, it might be worth it, but the only lives at risk are yours and the babe. I won't let you succumb to madness. I can't stand around, as I did today, watching you risk your life."

"But that means the monster wins."

"Look at me, Amora. The only thing that stays in my skull is keeping my wife safe. I'd rather be in Newgate than watch you riddled with pain. I've never paced or prayed more. I kept hoping your mother's whipped up brews or my cousin's commands would slow your contractions. I even sent for your vicar, but he wasn't available. I can't be this helpless again. I can't."

He plodded to the window, parting the curtains to let in the moonlight. She must have been sick for a long time.

"Remembering this fiend will hurt you." His posture sagged as he turned to face her. "You almost miscarried remembering the darkness he kept you in. Can't we let this alone for the child's sake? Don't you want this child?"

"What? How can I hope for something God will take from me?"

His lips twisted as if she'd rejected him. She wasn't rebuffing Barrington, just the notion that she could be fully happy.

"I see."

She wrapped her arms about her to keep the chill in his tone from freezing her. "I want to be strong again. Someone you can respect. That won't happen if I'm always lost to my memories."

"I didn't realize my opinion meant so much."

She pulled up her knees and tucked her head atop them. "It means the world. Always has."

He moved from the window and headed for the door. When his hand touched the knob, he stopped and turned again, catching her gaze. "I am just a man, a flawed man. If the need of my good opinion has kept you in bondage, let me help you. The one thing I had right the night we conceived this second miracle was to say you are mine no matter what. I meant it then. To love and keep you today and every day for the rest of my life, it *was* my dream."

Was?

"Whatever happens tomorrow, remember that God freed you long ago. He let you live through the Priory. He's kept you sane."

"Not permanently." She wrenched backward and ducked onto her pillow. "You saw that today."

A long, heavy sigh escaped. Maybe he felt every ounce of her despair. "God made you wonderful. And I know He wants you to look to Him for approval, not your ill-tempered, judgmental husband. I know He wants us to find joy."

Barr latched onto her gaze. He made his words slow and even. "I want you to find joy, even if we lose this child and have no more."

She turned her face away and imagined running hard and fast on Tomàs land. "I can't think about anything but proving to myself I didn't break my promise to you, that I didn't consent to the monster. With my lies to marry you, it would be too much."

Barrington shook his head. "What will it take to get

through to you?"

She rose up and pleaded once more. "Take me to the Priory. Be with me as I figure things out."

"I nearly lost you tonight, Amora. I can't do this again. I'm not strong enough. Promise me to stay in bed the next couple of days. Your body needs to recover."

Head down, Barrington plodded from the room.

He wasn't going to let her find the truth.

Why couldn't he understand?

Without the truth, how could they truly be free to love?

Something inside burned. Not the baby. A little higher, dead center of her heart.

Drop after drop leaked, but she kept her moans silent. She didn't want anyone to come crashing inside and think her more fragile.

Even a glass vessel couldn't be satisfied without the truth.

When they first courted, Barrington hated any other male, particularly the Charleton brothers, visiting Tomàs Manor. That's why he fought with the younger Charleton the night of the dowager's party. That's where his continued irritation at the vicar originated.

But needing to know wasn't about Barrington. It was about Amora and what she knew she needed to be whole. The truth would set her free.

Ignoring the tingle set low in her abdomen, Amora smoothed the bedclothes. It wasn't right to be so selfish, to risk all for what Barrington thought a forgone conclusion. But how was she to bring this baby, any baby, to term with so much uncertainty oppressing her?

She balled her fists. A hunger to be stronger whipped over her limbs. "God, if you love me, can't I know the truth without having anything else taken away?"

With a hand on her child, she ducked into her pillow and wept anew.

Chapter Three: The Truth & Miller

Barrington sat back in his carriage annoyed at himself for leaving Mayfair. Yet, how could he not resist his cousin's insistence or the man's humor?

Life had fallen apart again. All of Barrington's so called help for Amora lead to the same place, her in pain and potentially the loss of another child. He shifted in his seat. "We should head back, Hudson."

Hudson offered a smile. It was a cross between I'll-humor-you-you-witless-fool and you-amuse-me-you-witless-fool. "You need some fresh air, and there is something I must show you."

Barrington nodded holding inside his silent protest. Though Amora had rested a few hours without incident and without calling for him, she might need something. It wasn't quite 9:00 pm. Maybe she wouldn't awaken fretful and start those horrid contractions again. His insides tightened and twisted remembering her agony and how helpless he felt standing there knowing he'd allowed it.

"Cousin, you look terrible." Hudson's voice echoed in

the carriage. "Your wife is alive. The child to come, as well."

Poking down at his hastily tied cravat, Barrington's nose wrinkled at the hint of musk hiding within his perspiration stained shirt. "I look terrible. I feel terrible. I'm not fit for anywhere fashionable. If you have other plans, take me back to Mayfair. I need to be there *for her* or if Miller returns."

With a shake of his head, Hudson laughed. "Only so much you can do and stay upright yourself."

The man had paced as much as Barrington until Amora improved. Perhaps he needed to see the goons that Beakes brought into Mayfair. Miller was a dead man if they caught him. Well, dead again.

"And I don't do fashionable, Norton. I don't try to fit into places that don't want me either."

Oh, here comes the lecture. Barrington groaned inside. "Just when I remember to admire your good qualities, that irascible nature returns. Wait until your sister comes of age. You will do anything for her." *For her.*

That phrase again.

His attacker had said it, and so had Miss Calloway. Coincidence or calling card? Barrington brushed at his wrinkled waistcoat. Lack of sleep made him silly. Now he sought conspiracies, thinking the footpad who'd stabbed him was in league with the Dark Walk Abductor. He lifted his gaze back to Hudson. "Yes, anything for those you care about."

"You are right, Norton. I would do just about anything for Arabella, but she's not silly or taken by fashions either."

"When you run about town hunting the right silks and bonnets, I won't say I told you so, but I will think it. In fact, I'll practically shout it inside my brainbox."

Hudson frowned for a moment. "Well, I hear you do things for those you love. You love the Pharaoh's daughter, don't you? I believe that is how you described Miss Tomàs."

Barrington's fists clenched at such a stupid question. He tossed his head backwards upon the seat. "You know I do."

"I remember when you agreed to go to war to please your grandfather, you said Miss Tomàs would wait for you."

"Yes."

"And you said she didn't mind all the hard work it would take to get your practice profitable."

"Yes."

Hudson leaned forward, no doubt for the kill, the stabbing scalpel of the doctor's argument. "And every time, you look in the mirror and see your father's face, the man who put his own desires above his family, what do you say to your wife?"

Barrington straightened recapturing his cousin's gaze. He folded his convicted arms about his selfish chest. "Who is the barrister in the family?"

Hudson chuckled. "That would be you when you're not stewing. I wasn't thrilled when you said you were going to marry Miss Tomàs. Though her father was the best of men, he was Spanish, not English. It's hard enough for us to straddle where we fit in society. I didn't think you had a chance with such a mixture."

"Do you have a point? A valid one—"

"I'm not done. You've made your blended family work. Even gained friends in unlikely places. Just because the trail is rocky now doesn't mean this isn't your path."

Barrington blinked and wrinkled his nose again, but this time with suspicion. "What? Why say this now?"

"I may not have loved like you, but I see it. You love that little woman. And she loves you. Why else would she have put up with a great deal of waiting and supporting you?"

The blasted fellow sounded right, but that must be the battered hope dying in Barrington's chest. "What if she forgets that I love her? What if her malaise makes her not want our child?"

Barrington wiped his face. He shouldn't have voiced his frustration, but his conviction was broken when Amora couldn't admit to wanting this babe. "I've saddled my wife with a difficult pregnancy. I guess that makes me selfish three times over."

Adjusting his sleeves, Hudson cleared his throat. "Well, it's not like you can bear a child. And if you think she doesn't want the babe, then you are pretty stupid. I watched her when she finally settled. She cradled her stomach, absently rubbed her middle comforting the babe."

He wanted to believe his cousin, but Amora's mental difficulties might be too much to overcome. He loosened his fist, dusted the knee to his breeches. "She had digestive problems from all the teas and elixirs you and the good pharaoh had her drink."

Hudson slouched on his seatback. He looked wrinkled too. All but the vicar had paced and prayed for Amora's well-being. Where was the worm? And where was Miller? His friend was too weak to have simply left.

"Norton, you have made a team of loyal people. Your man James is. And so is Vicar Wilson."

The carriage stopped at the side of St. Georges. The

great portico filled the windows.

Wiping his spectacles, Barrington squinted at Hudson. "Why?"

"Go inside and see the vicar."

Bewilderment replaced the tiredness in Barrington's soul. He stood up and plopped on his hat. "I don't know what this is, but I'll not ask questions. I'll just go find out."

"Cousin, sometimes that's best. James will ferry me to my lodging then come back for you. Have a nice chat."

Nodding, Barrington climbed down then slogged into the church. This was ridiculous. He was ridiculous for thinking the vicar's absence at Mayfair was happenstance. No, the man was glued to them all because Barrington gave him an opening. Would he ever be rid of the one man who could love and care for Amora better than Barrington?

The admission made him nauseous. He gripped the back of a pew to remain upright. The thought of befriending the enemy made the nausea even worst, squeezing with the strength of a vise upon his innards.

He'd do anything for Amora, for her health and happiness.

Anything for her, including making a bigger fool of himself with her dear friend, the vicar.

Grunting impatient thoughts about casting the man into a lake of fire or off the highest cliff, Barrington took a couple more steps down the solemn aisle of the great church, then dropped into a pew box.

As if he'd been watching this display of indecision, Vicar Wilson appeared from a side. As he paced the length of the carpet runner, his hand clapped against the backs of the pew. Thud. Thud. With a lopsided grin, the vicar hummed.

The man could have been one of Barrington's childhood acquaintances. The naughty ones who held juicy secrets close to the breast but made no efforts in concealment. Usually those secrets were the latest scandal involving Barrington's drunken father. What did Vicar Wilson know?

Wilson stopped and tugged on his waistcoat with its sleek cut revers, then smoothed his dark jacket sleeves. "Awe, Mr. Norton, you came. Is Mrs. Norton any better?"

Releasing a silent groan, Barrington caught the man's gaze. "Yes. You know that. I would not have left her side if she wasn't."

The vicar's brow lifted as his smug smile grew. "Of, course. That is good of you. She needs your support."

"What else can a husband do? And since I've been dropped here by some conspiracy with my cousin, do you think it is possible to rid the foul air betwixt us? Perhaps it is best if we have no more, no more—"

"Distrust? Is that the word you are searching for?"

Surely there was plenty to be had. The man had supplanted Barrington as Amora's confidante. And did he gain his extensive knowledge of the Dark Walk Abductor's victims from just interviewing them? Could he have made sense of rambling as varied as Miss Calloway's? "You had my cousin waylay me. Speak."

"Mr. Norton, I am here to help your family. I think of them as my own. For their sake, we should be on better terms."

Shrugging, Barrington lifted off his top hat, settled it against the curve of his knee, and stared straight ahead at the painting of The Last Supper. Even at this late hour, candles illuminated the canvas at the front of the church. Amora, the painter, the lover of light would enjoy it, but it just reminded Barrington of her dousing that candle at Bedlam and her painful contractions. "The Last Supper. Do you suppose the Christ was out of options, forced to eat with friends and an enemy?"

"I'd like to think I am a friend. I don't wish to be an enemy. Your wife must think I am trustworthy or she wouldn't have shown me the escapee from Bedlam and potential murderer you liberated and stashed in your cellar."

True, true, true. What else could a stupid friend and husband do? Barrington nodded. Tossing his hat aside, he leaned back and crossed his arms. "Let's be about this. Why have you summoned me here?"

"I have Mr. Miller."

He almost jerked up from the seat. "What?"

"I've checked on your friend every day since I discovered him in the cellar. Whilst doing it, Mr. Solemn and I discussed how dangerous it was for your friend to be in your house."

Barrington wanted to drop his face into a palm for a hard slap, but couldn't give the vicar the satisfaction. Instead, he shifted against the hard pew. "Yes, it was stupid, but unavoidable."

"Sir, it would be the first place anyone would look, given your history of friendship to Mr. Miller and his sister." Wilson moved closer, only a pew or two away from choking or punching distance.

"How are you going to leverage this information, Wilson?"

"Will you listen? Last Sunday, I heard a runner bragging about smearing the smug mulatto, takin' him down a peg. I knew I had to act. When you and Mrs. Norton left for the appointment at Bedlam, I conspired with your cousin to move Miller from Mayfair."

Anger at himself for putting so much at risk battled Barrington's gratitude. He trudged to his feet. "Take me to Miller."

The man nodded and led Barrington into a tiny dark room in the lower level of the church.

Miller lay on a cot with blankets, snoring.

Part of Barrington's cares dropped away. Miller wasn't wandering the streets fogged or dead again from a vigilante's attack. He put a hand on the vicar's shoulder. "Thank you."

Sidestepping Wilson, Barrington sat on a stool by Miller's side. "Will you keep him here for a couple weeks? Long enough for his strength to be renewed to face the charges against him and for me to find the evidence to clear his name?"

"I'll do what I can. Church has always been a place of sanctuary. I didn't know I'd be conspiring in St. Georges to do so."

Gerald's weak eyes opened. He held up a shaky palm. "Take me now to magistrate. Caused too much…"

Barrington clasped and stilled Gerald's wavering hand. "Not yet. You have to give me a chance to build your case. I'm a little slower at discovering people's innocence these days. Sleep and listen to the…good vicar."

He stood and walked back into the hall. The musty smells of the almost century year old structure filled his nostrils as he leaned against the wall. His cousin, working with the vicar, could combat the ills a damp place like this could bring, but this was a much better place than Newgate.

In silence, he and the vicar returned to the sanctuary.

More tired now than before, Barrington dropped into his pew and retrieved his top hat. He rolled the brim, smoothing the nape betwixt his thumb and index. "Wilson, saying thanks is not enough. You allowed me to stay with Amora, keeping me from being dragged off to Newgate. Perhaps you are not all villain."

"I'm not. I suppose seeing the love of your life being cared for by another can be crippling to a jealous man. But, what else must I do to prove my love for this family?"

Such a foolish question to ask. Barrington couldn't request proof from anyone and who couldn't see how much the vicar had done for Amora and for him? "I'm grateful for all the encouragement that you've provided my wife. She's my heart. I'll accept her friends and come to better terms with you."

"That's all I want, Mr. Norton. I know you care for her deeply. Things will be well."

Care deeply? Barrington lowered his gaze from the vicar to the notches scratched into the pew in front of him. "The first time I saw her, she was painting. Her hair had loosened in the breeze. Her shawl and skirts fluttered like a hummingbird's wings, but she stood there painting as if lost to this world. For the first time ever, I wanted to be a part of her world not the one I was building. The long war made me forget and I made her live in mine."

"As a mulatto, I suppose you feel you have to build another one. I don't think you've failed her. You, me, we all must do our parts for her now. That includes keeping you out of Newgate. We need you here, finding the real abductor. I know you can."

If Wilson and Gerald weren't guilty, who was? Since

bringing Amora and her mother to London, Barrington had acted out of order, doing things against what he felt would solve the problems betwixt himself and Amora. He closed his eyes and listened to everything that felt right and moral inside, excluding that small bit of hope constricting his gut. "Miller must be turned in. He must stand against the charges. No one else can be put at risk for hiding him. I will defend him, and through my defense find the culprit."

"In a few weeks, he should be fit enough. Your cousin has told me how to administer his potions. I'll go with him and then send for you at the Magistrates."

"I'll take him in a fortnight. You've done enough, Vicar." Barrington paused, then fingered his lips to make sure they would still work when he said his final peace offering. "Promise me that if things do not go well, if I'm jailed or killed because of this, that you will take Amora from here. That you will love her and raise my child if he lives."

"Mr. Norton, we don't have to think the worst."

"The scales are gone from my eyes. You are a decent and annoying fellow. The dark walk abductor has power and influence. I feel it. The crown wants a conviction. They do not care whose family is destroyed. I need that promise, Vicar."

Wilson straightened, all the mirth leaving his countenance. "You have my word."

"I once thought that time should spin backwards to save Miller, the man whose life was shortened stepping in the path of a bullet meant for me. But time can't be stopped, and it's running out for Mrs. Norton's abductor. I shall solve the mystery of it, and I shall catch the cretin who has caused so much pain and death. Surely, that will return my wife's peace. Her serenity must absolve my soul."

"You do know she will have struggles with her sanity for the rest of her life? Can you help her? Or will you feel it another type of leash?"

Barrington had prayed and stewed on this since Amora flung herself off that high cliff. Maladies of the mind like the ailments of the late king could be ever present, always in the background like a predator waiting for a slip of the guard, for a momentary weakness to strike. He stood, donned his hat and glanced at the still sitting Wilson. "It takes great strength to love someone who's ill. One has to be stronger when she does not remember your love and patience. Maybe even saintly, when she turns away, goes to strangers. I'm a very, very strong man. Good evening, Vicar."

He trudged down the aisle and onto St. George's portico. The air was colder than before, causing the manured, off-putting scent of the streets to wane. He looked up at the stars in the sky and felt a strange peace. Maybe he'd been holding on too tightly to the plans in his heart. Letting go, thinking only of the next day and how he would bring hope to Amora, perhaps that was the way to keep this peace. It had to be. Barrington had no more options.

Chapter Four: The Quest for Truth

Two months confined within her Mayfair bedchamber with an easel and an unlimited supply of paint seemed like an incredible prison sentence to Amora, just for finding Sarah and for seeking the truth.

She swung her legs over the side of the bed and squished her swollen toes into her slippers. Maybe she'd venture outside the town home today. Was that too much to ask? Could Barrington and her mother be against her going with Mrs. Gretling to the orphanage? How could anyone be against orphans?

To be fair, she wasn't actually trapped in Mayfair. She could leave if she wanted to, she'd just have to get past Mama and Mrs. Gretling, and the enormous task of placating their fears of her falling...or worse.

And if Barrington were home, she'd have to battle his quietness. Though she was safe and the babe thrived inside, he remained silent. He slept in her bed, made sure she was awake before he left for his day, and always made it in by 10:30. With the exception of his laughter and shared confidences, he gave her everything she'd asked of him.

Did he fear another miscarriage?

A knock on the door made her flinch. She pulled her robe tight. "Come in."

Mrs. Gretling popped in with her polish rag. The scent of strong pine soap swirled from her bucket. "Good. You're up, ma'am. Does that mean the painting is done?"

Amora lifted her gaze to the easel by her window. "Almost. You can take a peek."

"Beautiful. The young lady is beautiful. Is she a friend from your old town?"

The picture displayed a smiling young woman with well-kept blonde hair coiffed into a tidy bun. Amora captured how she must have looked before the monster took her. Maybe someday she'd be able to give the painting to her. Amora smiled wide at the thought of helping Sarah. "Yes. Miss Sarah Calloway."

Mrs. Gretling's face pinched up. She dropped her cloth.

"It's not finished. Are you as critical as Mrs. Tomàs?"

"No, ma'am. It's lovely. It's just that name is similar to one of *his* victims. I saw it in the paper. Her family must be mortified to see their name open for public talk."

Amora dropped her head. She played with the ribbons of her robe. "Sarah's in the paper? Is she dead?"

"No, Mrs. Norton. It just listed victims of the Dark Walk Abductor and the horrors he's done to them."

"Then Miss Calloway must have this painting to bring her cheer. Something to keep her from being another lost soul, a name to be agonized or shamed. Women must stop paying for the monster's crimes."

Mrs. Gretling put her palm over Amora's fisted one. "I

didn't mean to upset you."

Stifled, Amora wanted to scream. Instead, she folded her arm over her head, pinned braids scattered everywhere, like her mind. "If everyone continues to fear upsetting me, I'll end up in the bed next to Miss Calloway."

Retrieving her rag, Mrs. Gretling backed up and shot to the door. "Sorry, ma'am. I think your mother wanted to know when you awakened."

The poor maid flew out of the room.

Amora chuckled on the inside at how fragile everyone thought she was. She couldn't be so easily broken. Barrington said she'd borne all the indignities the others had suffered. But was he also right in assuming her sanity would evaporate if she remembered being tortured by the Dark Walk Abductor?

The memories of being taken had returned, every detail clear. Her tongue salted as she recalled the pungent taste of pig scraps. Everything, even the sounds of his steps coming to her in the dark, had cemented into her mind up until the monster struck her, blaming Amora for Nan Druby's escape. When would she recall the worst?

Strength pulsed within her veins. She could weather it now, just as she could stand returning to the Priory. She wasn't so fragile. When would anyone see it?

She flopped upon the pillow and allowed the song that had been feeding her spirit to rise from her chest. "Through many dangers, toils, and snares I have already come. 'Tis grace that brought me safe thus far and grace will lead me home."

Barrington's wonderful song sounded good in her ears, in her heart. She had been through many dangers, but thus far she was safe and sound in her home. The home where she and Barrington conceived a miracle.

It felt true today, with her limbs fit and eager to exercise. She might've even gained some weight. Resting did help, but she couldn't be indolent anymore.

Pushing to her feet, she swayed a little. Something moved inside. She lowered to her mattress again and put her hand to her abdomen. A flutter wiggled. At first, it was sweet and light, then more pronounced. The babe said good morning. She should tell Barrington.

He'd attended her like clockwork, inside her chambers by 10:30 at night, out by dawn's light, always making sure to wake her and remind her that she was safe and free.

She tapped her thumb against his pillow. His scent of bergamot wafted to her nose. He slept beside her every night, and even held her if she asked, but part of him was missing. His conversation was dull, as if he made sure to say nothing upsetting. He must think her so fragile.

Angry, she balled her fist again and punched at his pillow. Barrington put her away from his heart, and she was at a loss as to why. What had changed since Bedlam? Where was the man so in love that he begged her to run away with him?

The creaking noise of the door hinge whined. Mama pressed inside. Mrs. Gretling fast on her heels.

Her abigail put her hands together. "Please don't ask her. Don't upset her."

"She has a right to know. Leave us." Her mother's voice sounded stern. Her face was pale, very pale as if something scared her.

Mrs. Gretling nodded and slipped from the room. Her

cheery, sherry eyes seemed wide with fright. The door shook as it closed.

"Did Gerald Miller, Mr. Norton's friend, take you? Is he your abductor?"

Was that the great concern? The latest gossip? Amora's heart returned to its normal rhythm. "No. Mr. Miller was not the one."

"But, the town is talking about the deserter who left his regiment returning to torture women. They say he dragged them to the Priory and…" Mama wrung her hands, her short boot heels ticked as she paced. "That's only a few miles from Tomàs Manor, close to the Norton's land. Were you held there? Of course you were. How else could you have crawled home?"

Amora swallowed. She didn't want to frighten her mother, but she'd not keep another secret. "I was there, but it wasn't Mr. Miller who did it."

Her mother plodded to the easel. She pushed at the ash-black curl peeking from her lacy mobcap and put her finger onto the canvas. "To think of the lives this man has ruined. He's about to go to trial and be defended by your husband. Doesn't Mr. Norton know what this could do to you?"

It made her heart soar, Barrington believing in Mr. Miller. But why hadn't her husband told her this? Was this why he was so distant? Big trials made him tense, especially the night before. Her heart warmed. Those were the times he'd let her care for him. "When is the trial?"

Mama pivoted with her hands on her hips. Her long burgundy gown swished with the effort. Breathing hard, she swiped at her face. "In a week. We should be out of London before the horrid accounts of his crimes become known and haunt you."

Too late for that. Her mother's cries touched her, pressing at the internal sack stored up with her own. It held tears for Sarah and Mama, for Miller and Barrington, even her child gone. All victims of the monster. Before any moisture could leave Amora's eyes, she arose, reached for Mama's hand, and pulled the good woman into her arms.

"Shhh. The damage is done." She stroked the woman's back. "I let my abductor steal more years by pretending nothing happened and fearing every moment that he'd return and hurt the ones I love."

Mama's cries were thick, wetting the collar of Amora's robe. "I wish I'd been strong for you."

With a final pat, Amora pivoted and stared at her painting. So much had been lost, too much. "I know what he's done to the others. He won't break any more of me. I've the grace of knowing my mind and somehow God led me home. I'm home, Mama, not in a cellar or an asylum."

The lady reared back, swiping at her eyes. "You do seem better, but speak to Mr. Norton. See if he can let us go back to Tomàs Manor, your real home. There, we can get you ready for your laying-in in peace."

"Is that some Isis ritual, Mama? I remember she's your goddess of offspring."

The woman shook her head, and lifted her tear stained cheeks. "What I believe has often been wrong. But, what I see in you is not false. It's true strength. I'd like to think that part of you is my contribution."

Amora rotated toward the bed. "My laying in is at least a month to come, but I should discuss this with Barrington. I'll speak with him tonight as soon as he returns."

"He's here now, downstairs in his study."

Squinting, she tugged her robe closer to her body, her entwined arms rested on the small swell of her tummy. "I don't understand. He's not at the Old Bailey or the Lincoln's Inn?"

"He rarely goes. The only client he's taken is Mr. Miller. It's almost as if he were afraid to leave you."

Barrington frightened? Not him. But not practicing the law, that must be about something else.

Her heart whimpered. His career must be suffering. Without trials, he would have to use his inheritance. Something he hated doing.

This was her fault. She'd leashed him to the house, to her. How ironic to gain the thing she'd always wanted then find it lacking. "I wanted to be a confidant, his helpmate. I don't need him to be afraid of upsetting his fragile wife."

She paced to the window and tapped the glazing. "I'd go to him now, but I don't think I have anything that fits."

Mama gripped Amora's shoulder's and spun her toward the closet. She flung open the door like it housed the prized Tomàs apples. "You do. I've seen to it."

Two new gowns, one in goldenrod and one in mint green hung inside. Amora waddled to it and slipped her palms over the sweet fabric. "I don't know what to say. I'm a swollen Cinderella, and you're my personal fairy."

The widest smile spread across her mother's lean features. "About time I did something for you. And it's good you're not leaving your happiness to others. Now, let me help you dress."

Though Barrington might not be able to see the color, the gown was lovely with pin tucks about the bodice.

Wearing it, she was sure to feel beautiful and confident. That would sustain her even if Barrington disapproved of her being up and about. She needed to believe she wasn't fragile. It was time to show him proof of her strength, proof they could go to the Priory for answers, do something to save Mr. Miller.

Pouring over the piles of notes for Gerald's trial made Barrington's eyes hurt. A month ago, he'd convinced his best friend to surrender to the magistrate and to trust the law, to trust Barrington. A week to go and he had nothing but a plan to exploit the testimony of the accusers, the bereaved families of the victims. How horrid for the best defense to be nothing more than an exploitation of misery.

He leaned back in his padded chair of tufted velvet and tried to readjust his back.

His spine of iron seemed to have rusted in place, curved from scouring law books and witness statements. Nasty business. If only the true villain could be found in Barrington's notes. His stomach soured as he thought of his friend.

Miller's speech had improved, but his memory of events was still sketchy. What happened when he confronted the Abductor? How did he end up in Bedlam?

Barrington had visited with him again this morning. Hopefully Gerald would remember something that would keep himself from dying for crimes he did not commit. An innocent man couldn't swing from Debtor's Door.

A knock upon the threshold made Barrington jump. He took a deep breath and willed his muscles to unclench. "Come in, Mrs. Gretling."

The door opened, but it wasn't the housekeeper. It was his very pretty, very pregnant wife. Her light-colored gown silhouetted her ample bosom and tucked about the beautiful swell of his child. His pulse ticked up. Her sleeping form draped in blankets hid the delight pregnancy worked upon her curves. Her very pronounced curves.

He laid his spectacles on the desk to make his vision blurry. No sense in unbalancing the apple cart with raw desire. "You should be in bed...in your room, resting."

She moved closer. Her lilac scent filled the air of his study tormenting his weak flesh. Then she leaned over him like a raw steak to a hungry dog. "I needed to see you."

Needed him?

No, not possible. Not in all the ways he wanted. Her full lips looked so serious pressed into a line. "I'll be up at 10:30. Surely, it can wait until time to retire."

She shook her head. "This can't wait."

He didn't dare put his lenses back on. It was far better to keep her at arm's length and her shapeliness blurry. "I'm sure whatever has you buzzing will keep. Perhaps you and Mrs. Tomàs can take a walk."

She moved to his bookcases. It was a little too far to detect if she were in distress so he put on his spectacles.

Her face held the widest frown. She flipped one of the spines down on the shelf. "Should I hop up here and stay out of the way?"

"No. You can see the shelf is full, and you know I like the tomes in alphabetical order. A is at the top."

She shoved the book back into place, then stared in his direction. "I see in the paper that Mr. Miller has been arrested. Were you going to tell me of his upcoming trial?"

"That's a second question. Your limit is one for today. Ask me this one tomorrow."

She folded her arms, creamy gloveless hands clasped her elbows. "Must you jest? I was fragile when we left Bedlam, but I'm well now. Tell me what has happened."

"Your vicar and my cousin got him out of here the morning of the raid. Wilson overheard someone bragging at St. George's about taking me down a peg. He hid him until Miller was stronger. Then I took him to the magistrate. In spite of things, your vicar's a good man."

Head cocked to the side, her lips were drawn into a tight O. "So when were you going to tell me?"

"You've had your one question, Lady Justice. Now, return to your room."

She rubbed her brow. "Be serious. Treat me as an equal."

"This." He waved his hand pointing at her and then himself. "What's between us is not equal."

She squinted at him. "Why are you being cryptic?"

"Then, allow me to be plain. You're doing everything in your power to bring this baby to term. I thank you for that. I'll make sure you are safe, and I'll continue working on a way to save Gerald Miller."

"If I can't help you, why am I here? I could be relaxing at Tomàs Manor, not stuffy London."

"I'll not allow you to go to Tomàs Manor and be within miles of the Priory. If you return to Clanville, I've no doubt you will try to go to the dilapidated structure."

The knock at his door drew his attention from the flush darkening her cheeks. "Come in."

James poked his head inside. "Sir, the new grooms are

in place and the new footman is ready on the carriage. We can leave as soon as you are ready."

He nodded to his man. "Thank you. I'll be along in a moment."

Swiveling his head toward Amora and then returning to Barrington, James backed out and shut the door tight.

Amora glanced toward Barrington. His cheeks had darkened. "Why so many servants? We are not showy people and the expense must be great."

"Yes, but necessary. The venom for defending Miller is great. I won't have you endangered. And I need to care too. I won't be caught off guard again."

"The attack on you? It wasn't a footpad. The monster is coming for you, like he said he would."

"No. No." He raised his tone to reassure her. He couldn't let her begin to fear for his safety. "It could have been a thief, but I think it was someone who doesn't want me to defend Miller. London wants a conviction. I'm in the way of that."

"But he said..." Her voice lowered to almost nothing. "He would strike out at you."

The ways the Dark Walk Abductor taunted his victims was horrible. How did he gain his knowledge of all the women? The villain had to be in a close circle. His stomach soured. They almost know him. Barrington probably knew him. He rubbed his temples. "I don't want you upset. I've taken more precautions. And I will return before 10:30. No need to fret."

Her lips buttoned. She looked down at her slippers. "You sound angry. I knew forcing you to keep my schedule would make you bitter."

Maybe he was a little stern, a little short from trying to find a clue that didn't put Amora's life in jeopardy. "I'm just tired, sweetheart."

"I know how you get with big trials. Let me help."

Barrington rose from his chair and marched to her, close enough to smell her maddening lilac scent. Close enough for her to crush his heart all over again. "Just bear these precautions. It has nothing to do with keeping a schedule."

She reared up, poking her slim finger along a rib. "I knew, I've always known, this delicate dance with a loon would make you hate me."

"Hate?" His agitation stirred, animating every corpuscle flowing in his tight veins. "Is that what you believe? Thinking of your dancing with danger gets me addled. I'm disturbed at how you take every opportunity to do something risky. From embracing a woman with chains, going down to a dark cellar to check on a man crying out in pain, or blowing out a candle and shrouding yourself in terror."

She poked him harder right along his scar. "I'm doing what I feel is right. I guess loons or victims don't get to do that."

Examining her uneasy breathing and her shuddering bosom, he softened his tone. "You think with your heart, not your head. You can't be in jeopardy again, not with our child."

Her cheeks darkened. Her chest gave a big I'm-not-going-to-cry-but-I-could heave, but she didn't move her hand from him. Her fingertips forced the organ caged behind his lungs to pound with need. "What's wrong with that, Barrington? I have a heart and I'm surely not thinking of rules every day."

He gripped her hand. Two months of dread over her enduring another moment of pain, of her losing this child, loosened his tongue. He could admit the truth. "Your heart has no room to love me or this babe I've saddled you with. Endure this pregnancy, then I'll let you be free."

Her violet eyes popped wide. "What are talking you about? I blew out the candle to protect you. I took care of Miller because he's your best friend. I did it for love."

"How can you love me and do things that will hurt my child?" He shook his head. "You think you love us, but you are ready to head to the Priory, probably with the foolish vicar. He's dying to help you with some scheme."

"If I succumbed to the monster, there has to be a clue there that will help you catch him. Don't you see? I'm the only who can."

It was true. She was the only one who might have seen the man's face, but what would that do to her? Madness, Miscarriage…Mayhem. He'd have to kill someone if she hurt ever again.

"You know this is true, Barrington. Will you let Miller be convicted because you won't let one victim not named in the papers help? I'm strong now."

The woman didn't understand, never would. He stepped away, slamming into his chair. "Do you think the other ladies were weak because they surrendered to the Dark Walk Abductor's demands? They weren't. Even a brave soul can break. The strongest person can give up."

"But I promise you I will not wilt."

"You also promised love and all your worldly troth. I don't need any more colorful paints." He chuckled and quickly shut his eyes to the hurt painting her face. "Going to the Priory solves nothing. Fear will grip you, tighten like a vise, squeezing away your reason and end the precious life you carry. I won't go through that again."

He clasped his fingers together, the veins along his hands bulged. He dropped them to his sides. "You gave me no choice at Bedlam. It took hours for your contractions to subside. You should have let me burn in Newgate rather than risk your health."

"Barrington! You can't be serious. Together we can save an innocent man. Your best friend. The man who took a bullet for you."

"I'm not serious?" He rooted through a drawer and pulled out a copy of her mother's legal agreement. With a dip of ink on his quill and a pat of his blotter, he slathered an X through a paragraph and signed the bottom of the parchment for September, a month after this babe's birth.

Every word of Mrs. Tomàs's separation document, the finality of it, weighed on his soul. If she did love him, maybe it would shake her from this course. Waving the page, he stood, plodded to Amora and placed it within her fingers.

She took it, but her hand shook as she read it. "What is this?"

"It's the signed separation agreement. It's effective in September, the month after your laying in. Then, you will no longer have to listen to your husband. This gives you the legal right to do whatever you wish."

She crushed the paper within her fists. "You're signing Mama's agreement? This must be some kind trick. We agreed to stay together to raise this baby."

"It wasn't we. It was I. I said we would, so now I say no." He took off his spectacles and rubbed his eyes. "You're not happy about carrying my child. With the unnecessary risks you're taking, we both know the odds of another miscarriage are high. You were in such pain after Bedlam. That should be all the evidence you need. No. This babe will be with me, so you can be free to find whatever will make you happy."

"You said you wouldn't take the baby."

"I'm giving you the freedom you wanted." He retreated, taking a step backward. He softened his voice as her eyes became glassy. "I will never keep you from our child. I'd love nothing more than for you to be content with us, but we both know that's not possible."

"I'm sorry." Her fingers burned his wrist when she clasped his arm. "This isn't necessary."

"I love you enough to let you go. It's the best thing to do for you. I keep hoping for the girl who danced in the wind as she held an easel waiting to show me her creation. The one who never lost patience when I couldn't see the colors. The impetuous Miss who snuck me into her father's study to play me a song. She's gone and so is her love. The monster has her and she won't run from him."

"This is against everything you stand for. It must be a joke, Barrington. You'd never give up this easily."

"Easy?" He spun her into the corner, leaning into her until his lips hovered an inch above hers. "There is nothing easy about shattered dreams. Hopes of sharing a family with you ripped asunder. But, I can't support something that will send you into madness or destroy this life within."

Her warm pants fluttered his cravat, touching the exposed flesh of his throat. It was as if she'd reached for him. His breathing intertwined with hers as their gazes locked. Why couldn't he stop loving her as easily as she'd stopped caring for him?

She slipped an arm about his neck, lowering his head. Claiming his lips, she stepped fully into his surprised arms. Instincts tightened his hold. His heart kissed her back with the same fire her affection always erupted.

Yet, this kiss wasn't like her others. This felt hungry, wanton, dizzyingly desperate. Her palms wove about his chest, her fingertips sliding against the taut muscles of his back.

Kerosene, whale oil, good old tar and flint, nothing burned like a woman who knew what she wanted. "Bar, we can do anything together," she said in his ear. "Let's go to the Priory and return with answers."

Gasping for sanity, he pried away from her willing arms. "That's very wrong, Amora. Didn't the Pharaoh tell you about playing with matchsticks and torches?"

"Maybe we need to be on fire to burn away everything keeping us from being of one mind. We both need answers. We can do it together."

"There will never be another for me, but I can't hold a ghost. A ghost can't be a mother to this baby, and I refuse to take this child to nurse at Bedlam." He put a hand to his mouth. He regretted his tone, but not his words. "I'll return by 10:30. Please be here, but I'll understand if you're not here."

She clasped his waistcoat. "Wait."

A button broke free in her hand.

He frowned at her, but he didn't try to take it from her shaking fist. Maybe she was trying to keep a piece of him to take with her as she did what she felt she had to do. "May the Lord keep you."

"I said wait, Barrington."

With her other hand, she claimed his palm and placed it on her abdomen.

One soft kick and then a hard one vibrated her belly, vibrating his hand. Their babe.

He should be a Neanderthal and take her by her twisted bun, sling her over his shoulder and keep her in bed for the final months of her pregnancy.

But he was just a barrister. A man of laws and logic. He bent and kissed her forehead, then rubbed his son good-bye. "I wish you both well. I pray for your safety."

Rotating to the hall, he left her in his study and headed straight for the door, almost forgetting to gather up his top hat and greatcoat. He slowed his gait, hoping that she'd reach for him one more time and agree to put their babe over her need for the truth.

He made it to the carriage unimpeded.

Resigned, he climbed inside and closed his eyes. He had an appointment to look at shipping manifests for the Duke of Cheshire. That and visiting with Gerald Miller would keep him busy. Anything to keep from thinking about Amora not being at Mayfair when he returned.

Chapter Five: The Quest for Unity

Barrington sucked in a deep breath of the stale Newgate air. The trial of the century would begin tomorrow, and he still hadn't developed a clear strategy of how to defend Gerald. The man was less than helpful, falling asleep as he prepared him for testifying. "Gerald, can you—"

Snores interrupted Barrington. How someone could be at peace in the old prison was beyond his reasoning. Yet, there Gerald lay as if confident he would be acquitted in the Old Bailey tomorrow.

Barrington wrenched at his neck and started to pace. From the brick wall to the bars and back, he tried not to think of Hessing's grin as he left the offices today. The man smelled victory. All Barrington smelled was defeat. It clung to the foul dampness in the air.

He stopped, pulled a handkerchief from his pocket, and mopped his brow. He tried hard not to let the damp smell of the air and eerie quietness remind him of waiting with Smith for the man's execution. The handkerchief made it worse. It smelled of lilac.

Amora and the Pharaoh had left Mayfair. The day of their big argument, he returned on schedule before 10:30 to an empty house. He gave her what she wanted, the freedom to destroy herself. Oh, how he wished she'd chosen to stay.

"Lord, let her be well. Let the babe..."

No more of this malaise. He stormed over to Gerald's cot, put his hands on his friend's thin shoulders and shook him. "For the love of God, remember something about the abductor. His face, His name."

"C-Could you stop?" Gerald tugged at Barrington's hands, but nothing save the Christ could break Barrington's iron grip.

Gasping for air, his friend lunged forward. "Stop r-rattling my bones. Going to be ill. S-sorry Mrs. Nor-ton left."

Barrington flung the man back to the cot and backed away. It had been a hard couple of days. Preparing for difficult trials always gave him a certain level of anxiety. Nonetheless, he'd become immune to the taunts on the street of "Accomplice" or "Helper of Evil." Even the news clippings and notes from victims' families shoved under his door at Lincoln's Inn had become an old hack.

However, his innards did sorrow over the ones without slurs. The ones just asking why. Why the renowned barrister would try to thwart justice? "Sorry."

Gerald stretched out on his cot. The thin mattress seemed to swallow the equally thin man. "Has she w-written?"

"No. Too busy visiting and seeing the sites. Probably missing the orchards... the cliffs...the Priory." He rubbed at his temples trying to eradicate the headache that had been with him since coming home to his empty house, save the housekeeper. Mrs. Gretling tried not to make things worse. She made beefsteaks, polished all the wood, but switching her polite smile from pity-on-you to stupid-man did not help. Barrington felt stupid. "I gave her a choice, and of course she took the dangerous option."

He clapped his hands together, summoning his mind from despair. "I need something to thwart Hessing. He's determined to see you hang."

"Y-your mentor?"

"Yes. I'm sure he put the inflaming stories in the papers, too. Maybe it is best my wife has gone. Being in this chaos could not be good. Tell me again what you recall of being found with Nan Druby."

Sitting up, Gerald cleared his throat. "I remem-ber a man, an older one with Vicar P-Playfair hovering over me. Then Cynthia."

Barrington started to pace again. The cogs in his mind stuck on Amora started to move, shifting and aligning the facts. "The old vicar was with Mr. Johansson? He's not mentioned in any of the reports, just the farmer, Johansson. Are you sure?"

Gerald closed his eyes and grunted. "Yes, the farmer and Vicar P-playfair. V-vicar and Cynthia put me in a wagon, a drey to be exact."

"Playfair knew everyone. He even sent his cousin, Vicar Wilson, to see about the victims."

His friend shrugged as he leaned back against the cold cinder wall.

Pounding over to the window, Barrington saw the Debtor's platform. The view from this cell was farther away than Smith's. At least his friend could be spared the agony of hearing the deathly preparations. "Playfair knew everything about Clanville. Maybe he knew you to be innocent. That had to be why he helped Cynthia hide you. Did she ever mention Playfair's assistance?"

Barrington spun back, leaning on the brick sill of the window.

Gerald stared ahead. His light eyes seemed to bore into Barrington's chest.

"What is the matter, man? Are you going to be ill, Miller?"

"You're missing a button."

He looked down and found the third button missing on his waistcoat. He must've put back on the one Amora ripped. Almost all his clothes were grey or off-black. Easy to do. "Yes, one is torn."

Miller reached for a mug from his small table and took a big swig. "I took a b-button from the D-dark Walk Abductor."

Barrington stopped fidgeting with the frayed threads of where the button would be. "Keep remembering. What happened to it?"

"It was in my palm. The indentation of it creased my palm. I don't know where it is. Norton, does this full story help? Does it do anything to save me?"

Barrington tried to put a smile on his face, put his lips wouldn't cooperate. "Every bit helps."

Gerald sat up and poured himself another mug. "You were never good at lying."

"When you get in the Old Bailey for the trial, I need you, my reserved friend, to be rowdy to show your innocence. Shout out questions. Ask for your freedom." Barrington plopped onto the bench.

Gerald's eyes widened as he peeked over the rim. "That will make the difference?"

"The jurymen and the judge will want to see that." Barrington kicked his feet out. "If none of the women testify against you, maybe I can convince the court that these charges are just hearsay. I could win this if I keep everything focused on the London abductions with no mention of the murder in Hampshire.

"You think you can do that, Norton?"

"If I were Hessing, I'd make sure that the testimony about the murdered girl being found at your feet be made known to the jury. That would convince them you are the Abductor. Once they establish that link, your conviction is assured."

Miller took another swig of his gin. He wiped his mouth with his coat sleeve. "They'll hang me?"

"If you're not hung here, you'll be tried in a month in the Winchester assize. The witnesses finding you with Miss Druby... You'll be convicted and hung there." Barrington gazed at the knotted thread still holding a button. The strands had lost their purpose, but they still clung to the fabric. They still had hope. *Lord, help Miller. Help me too.*

"You think Mrs. Norton might've testified if she were here? Do you think she could save me?"

Barrington rubbed at his face, pushing away the tired feeling in his eye sockets. "She couldn't say for certain you didn't kill the maid, but the strain on her would be too much."

With a big gulp, Gerald drank the contents of his mug. He rose and moved back to the cot. "I suppose you can't risk your wife. H-hold to loving her, though she d-doesn't do what you want."

Barrington felt his lips curl up at how his friend offered him encouragement even though Gerald could be sentenced to die tomorrow. "Miller, what can I do for you? Since I don't have a miracle to offer."

Gerald nodded his head and tucked beneath his blanket. "Then open up that book and finish reading St. John."

The cell door opened as Barrington started to pull out sections of his war bible. "Beakes, what are doing here?"

Mr. Beakes's mouth puckered to a dot. It was an almost penitent look upon the brash man. "Remember when I said it wasn't personal? I meant it. But, this involves Mrs. Norton."

Barrington's hand fisted beneath the scriptures. "Go on."

The solicitor reached into his brown greatcoat and pulled out a ribbon-wrapped paper. "Hessing wanted me to wait until the last hour to give this to you, but I couldn't. He's calling your wife as a witness. Now I know why you've been squirrelly about this business. I'm sorry."

A tremor set in Barrington's cheek as he took it. "My wife is with child. She can't testify. She's with child. Doesn't he care?"

"He only cares about winning, but as soon as I found out, I came to let you know." Beakes turned and headed to the bars, but stopped. "Oh, none of my men beat you. Be careful, like I told Mrs. Norton, London wants someone to pay for the Dark Walk Abductor's crimes."

"You told my wife?"

"Yes, at Mayfair. She sent me to look for you."

Barrington leapt to his feet almost beating his solicitor to the bars. "Miller, get some rest. I'm going home."

"G-God's speed."

He turned back and nodded to his friend, then headed to find his carriage. The joy in his heart turned ice cold, freezing into an iceberg. What condition would Amora be in, and how would they survive her testimony?

Chapter Six: Love Returned?

Barrington looked out his carriage window at the passing brick residences. In another mile or two, James would dump him onto Mayfair's steps. Why had Amora returned? And would she still be there?

Blasted Hessing. Was his mentor so heartless or did he want Barrington's defense to collapse? He must know that Barrington would do almost anything to prevent Amora from testifying. He shook his head at the lack of decency or civility from Hessing. The man wanted a show as much as he wanted blood.

Tossing his top hat to the floor, he eased his head against the seat cushion. An answer would come, something that would save Miller and keep Amora safe. He had to hold on to his faith, even when things were dark. God had been with them upon the cliff and at Bedlam. He could also see them through this gloom.

Finally, the carriage slowed then halted. As one groom opened the door, James climbed down, probably out of habit. His man tipped his tricorn and climbed back to the roof. The extra servants were something to get used to, but the stakes made it unavoidable.

Had he known Amora would return, Barrington would have had the house flanked with grooms. He'd use every cent of his inheritance to protect her.

Scanning the windows of the house, he found only the lights of the parlor glowing. Images of Mayfair ablaze the early morn of her miscarriage filled his eyes, forcing a hard blink. That day was a lifetime ago. She was stronger. Perhaps the babe was, too.

Scooping up his top hat, he flexed his fingers about the brim. How did she take the news of being made to testify?

Barrington's heart raced as he plodded to the door. Everything within him wanted to scoop up Amora and hold her close. He seized his key and forced the door to fly open.

Nothing seemed out of place. Was she in bed? Had she gone? When the sound of Amora's lithe voice stroked his ear, his pulse slowed, then ticked up.

A conversation emanated from the parlor, two feminine voices.

The unease in his gut wouldn't settle until he saw his wife. Almost running, he hastened to the room.

His breath caught seeing Amora. It had been less than a week, but it felt as if an eternity had passed. Before he could utter a word, his nose wriggled with the horrible smell of chrysanthemum. There sat Amora opposite her enemy, Cynthia Miller.

He didn't know which emotion to exhibit. Happiness because his wife was safe, anger at Cynthia sitting in his home, or befuddlement at the ladies engaged in easy chatter.

A grimace tugged at his lips. Anger seemed the best

course. "What is occurring here? Where's Mrs. Gretling? A footman?"

His wife tilted her head toward him. Her cheeks were pale, her lips almost smiling. Far from the agitation she normally showed around Gerald's sister. "I've sent everyone away. I wanted a chance to speak with Miss Miller in private."

Cynthia, dressed in clinging fabric, sauntered to him swishing her jezebel curves. "Mr. Norton," she pouted her lips. "I was at a loss myself receiving Amora's invitation, until she explained that you are separating."

"She did, did she?" He tugged off his gloves, tossing them with his hat to the show table out in the hall. "It's a private matter."

She smiled slyly and exposed her white teeth. The look had to be the equivalent of a female spider about to devour its mate. "I entered through the kitchen. None of your neighbors saw me."

He glimpsed at Amora who sat shrouded in an oversized shawl of silvery-blue knitted wool. Her expression of thinned pursed lips curled into a smile which sent a chill to his limbs. What was going on? His wife detested Cynthia. She'd be the last person to share marital difficulties. Oh, how he learned that lesson. Amora must be plotting something, probably something dangerous. The notion made his toes freeze within his boots.

Amora lifted her chin. "As I told Miss Miller, I no longer want to be the cause of your unhappiness. If I hadn't tricked you into marrying me, you would've been free to pursue her. This separation will make things convenient. I'm not fighting the attraction between the two of you any longer. At least I know her. Miss Miller will be good to our child when the babe is in London."

A tear filled Cynthia's light eyes. "Of course, I will. I love children. I would've kept mine if it had been possible."

Either Amora had completely lost her mind or the woman had a plan. This time he'd ignore the angst twisting his soul and trust whatever crazy thing she concocted. *Dear God, let her not have gone completely otherworldly.* He braced against the wall and folded his arms. "This is a trying time."

Cynthia waved a handkerchief, patting her stained cheek. "I'd given up hope about you, especially when you left me to stew in Newgate."

Amora splayed the fringe of her shawl over her palm. "All to appease me, I'm afraid."

"Is it true that you wanted me, Barrington, and have only been putting on a façade for your reputation?"

Before he let the cold truth fly from his clenched teeth, Amora swiveled toward him, her violet eyes staring through him. "I told Miss Miller, we've been running from the truth. I want you to be happy with a woman who loves you, but I also told her you'd only accept someone who'd been completely honest."

"Honesty is a good policy." He shoved his balled fist behind his back. She was leading Cynthia somewhere and he'd follow her lead. He'd trust Amora. "Have you been completely honest, Miss Miller? I refuse to be with a woman who'd lie for her advantage."

With violet eyes penetrating his heart, his wife's voice became low. "Never for advantage, but maybe for fear."

Cynthia stepped into his shadow, placing her hand on his elbow. "You seem nervous."

"Tomorrow is a very big day. Your brother's life is on

the line. I don't know how to save him."

"Go on, Miss Miller." Amora leaned forward. Her dainty slippers tapped against the floor. "Tell him."

Her voice dipped as she sang, "Ask me to forgive you."

He leveled his lenses. "I've done nothing wrong."

Cynthia leaned into him on tiptoes. "Well, do something now worthy of forgiveness."

"Mrs. Norton, I think you need to do a better job at selecting my mistress. This one is not taking the opportunity seriously. Miss Miller, take your coat and leave."

She gripped his lapel. "What is it you need to know?"

"You claim to love your brother, but you left him to stew in Bedlam drugged. Why?"

She stepped back, sputtering. "I-I-I-I'd never let anything happen to him."

Lies, all lies, but it was time to press her for answers. "But you did hurt him. You hid him. If he'd faced the charges in Clanville and defended himself, he might be freed of this. The Dark Walk Abductor stopped almost to the date of Miller being put in Bedlam."

Amora stood up, clasping her elbows as if she were cold. "Tell him about the monster's button. She took it from Mr. Miller's clenched palm."

"Yes, I have it. It's marked with a crest. Will that prove his innocence?"

Gritting his teeth, he glared into the singer's darting eyes. His innards seethed. "You know who the abductor is?"

Cynthia released his lapels and took two steps. Her voice was tiny like a mouse's squeak. "Don't look at me as if I'm evil. We both know only one woman in this room loves you."

Head high, Amora marched close. Glorious dark hair, woven into a neat bun, shadowed her long neck. The broad cloak hanging upon her shoulders shrouded her form, allowing no glimpse of the forceful curvy lady beneath. "Why not tell the man you love how you knew his fiancée was imprisoned in the Priory? How you left me there to die?"

Cynthia's rouged cheeks paled. The squeak became higher, blurting in fast trumpets. "I didn't. I wouldn't. No, Barrington."

The viper pivoted toward Amora. "You said I was here for him, not to expose me to his hatred." Cynthia's voice shook. "I don't have to stay and listen to this. I—"

Barrington grabbed her wrists before another falsehood was uttered. "Answer the question or I'll tell the magistrate you are in league with the true abductor. You blackmailed the abductor because the button identifies him. Isn't that how you got Miller's care paid for? That is why Vicar Playfair knew your brother was innocent. That's why he helped you smuggle him from Clanville to London after the Druby murder."

"Yes." Tears fell from her soulless eyes. "I hated Amora for having you. But, I'd never leave her in the Priory. You have to believe me." She wrenched free. "I'll bring my proof."

Amora rubbed her temples. "Proof? You kept the monster's secrets all this time?"

Cynthia sank to the floor, scrambling to her cape. "No more abductions happened once I found out. I took steps to make sure." Thick sobs mixed with her words." I...am not...a bad person."

Barrington led Cynthia toward the door. "Bring the button tomorrow to clear your brother's name. It's your only hope of his acquittal. Hessing's out for blood. If you play us false, you've put the noose on your brother's neck."

She trudged to the hall with waterworks and shaking shoulders. All the trappings she'd used to endear herself to him. "I'm not a bad person."

His gut wrenched, knotting at the lies he'd swallowed from Cynthia. He propped the door open. "In the witness box tomorrow, bring your false smiles for the jurymen. Focus your forked tongue on London. Don't mention Clanville or the milkmaid's murder. With that button and your acting, maybe your brother won't hang."

The wench ran.

Barrington slammed the door. "All these years, I should've trusted your instincts."

Amora heaved a long breath and nodded. "I should've trusted your love and told you everything the moment your rode back to Tomàs Manor from the war."

His pulse raced. His heart opened at the smidgen of hope he heard in her resolute voice. Staring at his fingers, he took off his tailcoat and laid it over the arm of the sofa. His hands harbored guilt as well.

"A year ago, I trusted her. I sent you home with that woman from Lord Cheshire's ball. Could her prattle have caused you—"

"It didn't help." Amora's soft voice penetrated his skull. "I don't want to think about what might have been. Not anymore, only the future."

He wiped a hand through his hair. "She knows who did this to you and never said a word. I should haul her back and make her confess the name tonight."

"No." Amora's tone sounded confident, decisive. "Cynthia won't tell unless she thinks it will gain her something. She needs to bring the button tomorrow. Let's not focus on things we can't change. It's the night before your big trial, your biggest yet."

"Hessing wants you to testify. I won't permit it."

"Saying the truth, admitting it to the world wouldn't be the end. Maybe it would be a beginning."

He couldn't think of her standing in the witness box, with all of London glaring at her, judging her. Instead, he drank in the sight of his confident wife. Smooth complexion, wide eyes, her cheeks looked a little fluffier. He edged closer, his heart beat faster and faster. "Why is the house empty?"

Amora warmed in Barrington's gaze. She counted the rise of his chest, wondering if his pulse raced as hers did when he stepped near. "I remember how you get before the big ones. You like it quiet."

"So, you enjoy watching me get all worked up?" He folded his arms. His voice slowed, lips flattening. "No other reason?"

There were plenty of reasons: Missing him, unfinished yearnings, the trial of an innocent man. She didn't know where to start. And how could she testify without Barrington's support?

He took off his spectacles. "Cynthia could be dangerous. Where is your mother? The infernal vicar?"

"Mother's with the Wilsons. I wanted Cynthia to be at ease. She admitted to having the button, and I got her to say it to you."

With a tug to his onyx waistcoat, he bounced out of the room and bolted the door. "So, you're not done taking risks?"

"I didn't go to the Priory. I started to, but your button.

I put in my sack of notes. I saw it every morning when I read the encouragements you wrote. I couldn't risk everything without you."

He stopped at the threshold and stared, dumbfounded. "You didn't go?"

She directed him to the sofa. "No, I decided it would be safer to bring the monster to me, to us. I felt she knew more than she ever said. So, I was her advocate tonight. A wife willing to look the other way. Cynthia does love you in her own twisted way."

Barrington hung his head, slumped his shoulders and dropped onto the cushions. "It's good to be loved by someone, even if it's poisonous. Sorry."

She swallowed, took a deep breath, then released the words burning her tongue. "I don't want a separation."

He lifted his countenance. His gray eyes danced, then slimmed to dots. "It's not necessary. You can visit with the babe anytime you want when he's with me, but you are right about London. It might be best if he stays with you at Tomàs Manor. In your care, he'll thrive. I remember how you made good old Mr. Tomàs's pianoforte sing. Our child should grow up knowing your arts and your music. Just keep your brave spirit restrained at least until he's of age."

He thought her brave and competent but was still letting her go? Chest aching, she focused on the planes of his face, the tremor vibrating his cheek. "I decided I want my husband. And he needs to know that."

"I'll draft new separation papers after the trial sharing custodial care of the babe." He seemed to reach for her hand but stopped. Only a few feet separated them. "You should be in bed resting. I could try to persuade Hessing to change his mind, but you are his principal witness."

"You're not listening, Barrington."

He took a final step with his long legs and put his hands on her shoulders. His fingers curled into the fringe of her cozy shawl. "Then say it plain."

Not releasing his gaze, she nodded. "I want you, Barrington, probably always have. I didn't feel worthy of your love because of what happened. I lacked faith in us. I wasn't fair to you, hoping you'd make everything better, and you had no understanding of the problems. I'm sorry. I still want you to love me. We can do anything if we are together."

He pulled a strand of fringe, then another. His warm palm cupped her shoulder, wilting the cap sleeve of her simple bodice. With a gentle push, he freed her of her shawl.

Sinking on one knee, he mumbled to himself. Maybe something about God and being blessed. His fingers circled the swell of her abdomen. He kissed her middle and held her close, his face buried in the buttercream fabric of her dress.

His lingering breath heated her insides. She shivered. Oh, how she missed his arms.

With a shaky pinkie, she traced his hairline smoothing back the dark curls and silvered locks. His warm, fragrant bergamot spice filled her nostrils overtaking the tawdry singer's chrysanthemum. "With my head clear, I dream of you. I can see the future you wanted for us."

His voice was low, garbled. "You're here. The baby's here. We are of one mind at last."

A tear weighed on her lashes, and she blinked it away. "You were right about the Priory. It doesn't matter, nor do the hurts of the past. Perhaps, when the child's not at risk, maybe we can go together."

"We'll see." The hold on her waist didn't slacken. His words vibrated through the layers of muslin and silk down to her skin. "How did you know about Cynthia?"

"She always seemed to tease at a secret. When I tore your button, I remembered Miller saying he clutched one from the monster. I hoped with the right incentives she'd admit to it, and she did."

"My wife, a brave foolhardy woman. What am I going to do with you? And Miller's trial, how do I keep it from destroying us?"

"That's tomorrow. I'm focused on right now. I hurt you, and I don't know how to fix it." The sob pressing against her lungs, the pain that nibbled at her conscience every night this past week, stabbed and poked until it broke free. Water flooded her cheeks. "I must fix it."

Not letting go, he stood. "It's fixed." Keeping one hand at the small of her back, he used his other to lift her chin. He bent and allowed his mouth to tickle her jaw, drinking her tears. "No more sadness in Mayfair. This needs to be a place that means happiness and safety, just like Tomàs Orchards. In fact, I have something to show you."

He hoisted her in his arms and carried her from the room to the stairs.

Her pulse raced as he reached the landing of her bedchamber. Had he forgiven her that quickly?

When his foot left the steps and he approached her door, her heart missed a beat. Would he shelter her in his love? She gripped his lapel and caught her anticipating smile reflected in his spectacles. It would be wonderful to have his love once more, before tomorrow, before everything changed again.

"Can you get that candle?" He angled her toward the

wall sconce. "I don't want you in the dark."

She clasped the precious light and settled again on her perch against his strong chest.

He turned, not entering her bedchamber. What?

As if swirling in a cyclone, he spun and took the next set of treads leading up to the attic. The pit of her stomach clenched. Disappointment riddled through her. "Where are we going?"

"Patience." A grin set on his face. "I've learned that lesson, a great deal of it this year."

The frail light barely illuminated his boots, but she wasn't afraid. Pressed against him, there was no safer place to be.

"My lovely sweetheart." His words kissed her everywhere. "Light the sconce."

She blinked and did as he asked. The attic? What was he up to?

He set her down, took the candle from her, and slipped inside. Soon light seeped from the cracks about the door. He returned and ushered her in.

Her mouth opened. No more trunks or piles of old furnishings. The room had been remade, clean with vibrant pink and green paint on the wall.

"Come." He held out his hand to her.

She noted the pianoforte in the corner, then the easel by the large attic window. The setting sun beamed down upon it and the wide array of pink and puce pillows covering the floor. It looked made for a celestial picnic.

A mural stretched along the longest wall. It was a Pippin apple tree with bright red and striated fruit.

She put a hand to her hip. "Can you even see the colors of this orchard?"

"I see what I need to. The smile on your face is worth

a rainbow."

"When did you do this?"

"Most of it was done the morning we went to Bedlam. I wanted to have something ready to give you cheer when we returned from asylum. Then the chaos with Beakes and..." He bit his lip. "More was done the weeks you rested. I need the vision in my head complete."

She clasped his arm, pleasure rippling through her. "Is it?"

"Almost." He walked her to the pianoforte and set her upon the bench. "Your mother returned your painting. I thought I might try to get you to play."

Gobs of sheet music lay atop the fine cherry wood box. The instrument shined with waxy polish. "I didn't have the heart to play Papa's. Maybe since this instrument is here in London, I could."

Barrington traced the arch of her neck. "This is yours."

She tapped a few keys. Closing her eyes, she hit a few more.

The notes turned into Haydn. A march, one of power, fell from her fingers. The gait, the pitch was perfect. No sadness.

Memories of her father swirled about, joyful ones. She played the tune again. The crescendo surged through her palms making the ivory come to life.

"Papa would love this." She lifted her hands and clapped. "I hadn't played since the last time with him."

Barrington hugged her neck, his powerful forearms wrapped against her shoulders. "It's fitting you do so now with this papa-to-be."

She turned into him. Her lips on his throat must've caught him off guard.

He bolted upright and pushed at his hair. "I just wanted you to see this. It's getting late. You should rest."

"I don't feel like sleeping. Tomorrow could end everything."

His smile disappeared, and his gaze fell away.

Her heart clenched, breaking. Had he always been this vulnerable to her? Had it been there all along undetected because of her guilt, the weight of her secrets?

He had to know how much she loved him. She stood and touched his forearm. Sparks heated her skin as her thumb slipped along the pulsing vein at his wrist. "The document you signed is very thorough. I may not be allowed to sit up and talk with my estranged husband." She looped her arms about his waist. "It might forbid this." She planted a kissed on his throat.

"I didn't sign away those rights." His palms went to each side of her face. "Or this either." He dipped his head and brushed his lips against hers.

The touch was soft, almost distant. She pressed closer, tilting her chin to give him access to her neck. Her hands dug underneath his waistcoat. Could she hide inside his pocket and avoid tomorrow?

His kisses deepened, spinning her like threads on a weaver's wheel. His fingertips traced the lace of her bodice dipping in and out from silk to skin to silk again. Melting against him, she loosened his cravat, the buttons of his shirt. She had to feel the battle hardened muscles beneath. The need to taste his strength etched in her mind. That would sustain her when she testified in the witness box.

He stilled her hand against his beating heart. Seventy-two, no eighty beats throbbed against the lifeline of her palm. "We should stop. You must rest. I should too.

Miller's trial will be brutal."

"I remember how you get before a big day in the Old Bailey." She plodded to the mounds of pillows, and sank into the puffy masses. Her slippers flew into the air as she lost her balance.

He was at her side before she could count rafter beams. "I had pictured us on these pillows, but I guess it's a better vision than practicality." He took her hand and hoisted her upright.

Flattening and beating a few into submission, she smoothed her pinkie against a satin cushion. "You pictured us here?"

"Yes, but your hair is loose." As if saying it aloud, stirred him into action, his hands dove into her chignon. Pins and curls fell everywhere as the braid erupted. "Now the picture's complete, except we're both still dressed. Something to look forward to."

A sigh blasted from his lungs. His face darkened. "I don't know how to save Miller, but a strategy will come."

"You're anxious. You can't settle. I remember." With a tug, she freed his shirt and planted both hands along his ribs. "Then you'd come home to me."

His silvery eyes widened. "That's what you remember? Is that why you said you love me? To take my mind off my troubles."

"I remember every time. It took my troubles away too. Take them away, *now*."

"Now?" The question came out pitchy and high. With a cough, he lowered his voice to his normal octave. "Now?"

"Yes, I'm strong enough. And, I'm desperate for you." She planted her mouth against his. This time she had no intentions of being deterred.

Nodding, he grinned and claimed her kiss.

Buttons and pins released as he swept aside everything but her corset. His arms wrapped about her and eased her onto the pillows. "So beautiful and all mine."

She pushed a dark lock from his temple. "Tell me you will love me no matter what."

He flung his spectacles to the side. "Yes."

"Even if I again do something that angers you? Even if I crumble when Hessing makes me testify?"

"Hessing." He pulled her close, pressing her into his chest. Taking her with him, he fell against the pillows. "The blasted fellow doesn't just want to win. He wants to crush me completely. I'll talk to him again before court starts. See if there is another way."

"No. It's time for the truth to be out. Use my testimony to help Miller."

"But the memories, the effect on your health." His arms tightened about her as if she'd disappear.

Maybe she would.

The strain could send her into madness, but the truth had to reign.

Something had changed in her heart. It was subtle, growing daily. God filled her with expectation, amazing grace. The life growing and kicking inside would live even if her mind disappeared, she knew that now.

Barrington stroked her hair, even as he muttered something harsh, like 'smashing Hessing', under his breath. "Sweetheart, rest. Get some sleep. Tomorrow, I'll have some idea how to save everyone. God hasn't forsaken us. How could he when He's returned your love."

Tears clogged her throat, but he had to understand. "Be with me tonight." She swallowed and leaned into his chest. "Let me know all of your love, so no matter what, I know I've found happiness, utter complete happiness, one last time."

His pupils darted, then settled. "I love you and won't ever stop. Never." He claimed her lips. His ardor was slow, the strokes to her skin tentative. His breath upon her cheek, a whisper.

But he wasn't a tentative man.

With each kiss, he stole more air. The sweetness of his love overcame her. She shut her lids and swayed with the wind of his movements, trembling within the eye of the storm and the strong arms surrounding her.

Not for one minute did she feel fragile, spent, or afraid.

Chapter Seven: The Trial of The Century

Barrington tugged on his horsehair wig making it fit more snugly at his ears. He took a quick breath and smoothed the lace bands of his collar. The sweet nosegay wafted by the clerk at the beginning of the session still freshened the air at the Old Bailey. He peered at the growing crowd in the gallery. His stomach turned, clenching as he counted. The spectator's numbers grew to hundreds.

All here to witness the Dark Walk Abductor's downfall, but the penalty would befall three: Gerald, Amora, and her babe.

A sigh forced its way out, heating his nostrils. His lungs squeezed at the wave of helplessness filling his chest.

Barrington straightened and turned to the front of the court.

Justice Burns leaned forward in his chair. The glow of the desk lamp reflected on his robes. "The jury has found you guilty of the charge of theft."

The judge's clerk appeared and put the black cloth

upon Burn's head. "Make the prisoner rise."

Three hits with a baton made the man in the prisoner box stand to his full height.

The opposing counsel should go to his client and bolster him for the sentence to come. Barrington leaned over to whisper his advice when he caught sight of a vision in the gallery.

Amora led by Vicar Wilson and Mrs. Tomàs settled into a seat.

His wife left him in the attic to awaken alone. No good byes or final pleadings. She probably knew he'd attempt to talk her out of coming.

Yet, she did leave their separation paperwork laid neatly by his boots. Scrawled atop the parchment were the words, "Burn at your earliest convenience."

Which he did.

With a wave of Burn's hands, he silenced the crowd. "The defendant," the judge said, "you will be led back to jail from whence you came and stay within its walls laboring and repaying your debt for the next three years."

The gallery erupted, some hooting, others weeping. The Bow Street Runner who brought the indictment jumped up and waved.

"Who will feed m'children?" The sentenced man sobbed and clutched the iron rail of the dock.

The gaoler tugged almost in rhythm to the spectator's chanting, "Three. Three. Three."

The bailiff joined the gaoler. Each clutched a scrawny shoulder of the convict and dragged him out of the courtroom.

A hush soon covered the place again.

As the people parted, Barrington saw his petite wife

again with her raven hair swept up in a neat chignon. Like a fruited cake covered in bliss icing, she was topped with a fine bisque bonnet. The scalloped neckline of her dark yellow gown accentuated the curve of her full bosom and the delicious flair of her hips. A lacy shawl draped her elegant neck and framed the gentle rounding of her abdomen. Amora. His wife and child. Would the three know a day of peace? *God, allow us to find a home together, intact.*

He blinked his eyes, but couldn't take his gaze from her. His heart beat a thousand times a minute. He fingered the air tracing her silhouette, circling her lips to his.

A pounding came from behind.

The reality of the court proceedings interrupted his woolgathering.

Justice Burns slammed his hand against the desk. "Bring in the next prisoner."

Hessing flopped into the seat nearest Barrington, the place the two plotted strategy and worked together on so many cases. How could his mentor conspire against him?

Father, my heart cries out to you. What am I to do?

"Don't look so grim." Hessing chuckled. "If you beat me, you'll know how good you are." His blue eyes flickered. He leaned over the table jutting out his double chin. "Remember, what I taught you. It's the stewardship of the law. There are no enemies or friends in the Old Bailey, just facts and persuasions of justice."

The older man pulled out three pieces of paper and shuffled them. "Your wife's testimony is on top."

Barrington's hands shook as he read. Finding no gory details among the circumstantial information he released a breath. Could the woman again be aiding Barrington by providing scant details?

"It was a shock to discover Mrs. Norton's connection with the case from the administrator of Bedlam." Hessing smirked at him. "If your client admits his guilt, there would be no need to call your wife to the box. I would do that for you."

"As much as I'd like to spare her any pain, my client is innocent." Barrington gritted his teeth. "I suppose we'll both have to earn this win."

With a tug on his silk robe, stomach protruding, Hessing picked up the briefs. "Wouldn't have it any other way." He trudged down to the far end of the bar for another seat."

The gaoler entered and led Gerald Miller to the stand. He looked thinner, if that was even possible. But, wore a new brown tailcoat and buff breeches. Cynthia must've bought the clothes to spruce him up.

The bailiff approached the judge and read from a long piece of parchment. "Gerald Miller is charged with the abduction and assault of Miss Sarah Calloway of London, and the abduction and assault of Mrs. Anna Tantlin of Cheapside."

A horrible rumble erupted from the crowds. One middle-aged man shouted, "Abductor!"

Another followed. "Dark Walk Abductor! He's taken more than two. Killed more too."

The whole gallery began to chant, "Abductor."

Amora patted her forehead. Could the noise or the heat be affecting her or the babe?

Barrington swatted his own brow. The Lord made him a barrister. He'd use everything in his soul to destroy the case so soundly, the woman who owned his heart, his future, wouldn't be called to testify.

Amora sat back in her chair in the first row of the gallery, closest to the barristers' desk. From here, she could count without strain the stacks of legal documents, the rolls of ribbon-tied briefs scattered along the semi-circular table, and the uneasy breaths lifting from Barrington's chest.

Poor fellow. He must be in agony about Gerald. And probably over her testimony too.

She glimpsed down upon the heavy pleats of her bodice. Barrington, the baby, they'd have to understand. She had to do this. She finally knew and trusted her own strength.

Lord Burns slurped from his gilded cup then lowered it, hitting a candelabra nearby. Moving both, he scowled. "Mr. Hessing, proceed with your questions."

"Yes, my lord." Barrington's mentor arose from his chair and stopped in front of the jurymen. "Gentlemen, I will begin with witnesses to the atrocities. Loved ones who can attest to Miller's guilt. I call Mr. John Calloway."

The older man lumbered to the witness box, swore to Almighty God to tell the whole truth, and kissed the Bible. Hessing traipsed to the front of the court. He stood a few feet from the rectangular frame holding Sarah's father. "Tell us about your daughter's abduction."

Amora blocked out the poor father's thick Irish brogue and looked at Mr. Gerald Miller. Barrington's friend looked so frail and thin. The panel hanging over his head amplified the knocking of his knees. He must be as nervous as she.

Closing her eyes, she focused on the peace of Tomàs Orchards and the sweetness of Barrington's affections. If she lost her wits, at least now she knew he still loved her and she, him. Hopefully, he'd treasure their one perfect evening if tragedy struck.

Samuel's arm brushed hers. "Are you well?"

She nodded, then slipped her fingers along his sleeve until she clasped his palm. "It's good to have my friend near."

He squeezed her hand within his. "A job I relish."

Mama's eyes were shrouded beneath the shadow of her large bonnet. Was she praying?

With a pound, a fist slammed against wood. She lifted her gaze and watched Justice Burns hit his mahogany desk again.

"Quiet!" Justice Burns raised his arms, signaling to the crowd. "Who shall be tossed out through the rear today?"

This time the crowd heeded. Silence swept over the gallery and the jurymen.

The judge leaned toward the witness box. "Mr. Calloway, please continue your testimony."

The old man, Sarah's father, gripped the edge of the polished wood framing the paneled stand. "The Abductor took my girl from the Dark Walk, hit her with his hands, forced himself upon her."

Barrington's mentor rounded close. "So, it is your testimony that your daughter, Miss Sarah Calloway, was taken from your possession without your consent?"

Mr. Calloway hung his head. His straight back sagged. "Yes." His voice clogged with sobs. "Yes. The surgeon verified she'd been assaulted."

"And after this vile act was done to her, the poor maid was found babbling in a ditch near Clanfield, Hampshire, over three hours from here?"

"It is so." Mr. Calloway bent over and clutched the

edge of the stand as if to keep himself upright.

Mr. Hessing spun and faced the jurymen. "Is it your testimony that Sarah Calloway was taken and abused by the alleged Abductor of Dark Walk?"

"Yes, sir. And he," Sarah's poor father pointed toward Mr. Miller. "He should die for what he's done."

The clicking of tongues and rising whispers rushed across the audience as Barrington's mentor sat and smiled like a hungry alligator.

Her husband stood, turned from his friend and gazed at her. His palm gripped the lace band of his collar as if he had forgotten what he was doing.

He turned to the witness. "My heart hurts for your daughter, for all the women affected by the Dark Walk Abductor."

Mr. Calloway looked down. "She was a good girl. She didn't deserve this."

Barrington half-pivoted. "*Was?* Miss Calloway is still alive, is she not?"

"Yes, what's left of her."

"Sir, describe what's left of her."

"I... Her mind is gone."

"Doesn't sound as if you've had a chat with the young woman in a while. Tell me, sir, do you make time for her concerns?"

Chuckles filled the air. Was Barrington purposely baiting the man?

The witness jerked his head up. "I work hard to protect the interests of my family. I'm not an infidel."

"An infidel?" Barrington's gaze seemed pinned to her fevered brow. "Work is never more important than family. Every man needs to know that time is well spent protecting his loved ones."

A lump lodged in her throat when he turned back to Mr. Calloway. Barrington's heart had moved so far. Mr. Calloway yanked at his sleeves. "I'm not on trial. Your troll of a client is."

Adjusting his spectacles, Barrington looked at his pile of briefs, flipping through the leaves of paper. "When your daughter was returned, did she describe what her abductor looked like?"

"No. She was too full of tears. Too grieved to talk more about it."

Putting his hands behind his back, Barrington paced closer to Miller. "Then how can you claim my client is guilty?"

Mr. Calloway stomped his foot and grunted. "I see the evil in his eyes. He's guilty."

Barrington reached up and put a hand over Gerald's face. "What color is evil?"

Sputtering an obscenity, Mr. Calloway shook his head. "I don't know. Maybe gray like yours."

A smile bloomed on Barrington's handsome face. "Before the attack, was your daughter a petite shriveled thing?"

"No, she was tall and quite fit." Mr. Calloway's voice sounded softer, filled with anguish.

Unlike Sarah, she still had her reason and a last chance at happiness. None of that could be Sarah's, not as long as she was locked away in gloomy Bedlam. There had to be something to do to restore hope for Sarah and Mr. Calloway. Amora's heart clenched, then seized on a new thought of helping those like her.

"So your daughter was tall and quite fit?" Barrington marched back to Gerald and gave him a shove.

The fellow slid to the other side of the stand and

clutched the rail. A bewildered look crossed his face as his chained arm rubbed his ribs.

A roar erupted from the gallery. Even the jurymen laughed.

"Mr. Norton, stop with the antics." Justice Burns leaned upon his desk. A deep frown etched below his pointy nose.

"Sorry, my lord." Barrington lowered his voice. "So you don't think she could've fought off my client, this bag of bones? As you can see it would be quite easy to do."

The crowds snickered again.

Mr. Calloway's cheeks burned scarlet. "You tryin' to say she went willingly? My daughter is not some doxy."

Barrington pivoted back to the witness stand. "No, but that's what you thought. Is that why you didn't come forward until the charges were announced?"

"He needs to pay. Can't you see that?" Mr. Calloway cleared his throat and tugged at his flaying cravat. "I... I want the scum to pay for what he did."

"Maybe we should all be on trial. For not believing the victims until their numbers grew." Barrington sighed loud and hard.

The deep resonance of his timbre sent a shiver down Amora's spine. Was that guilt in his voice? She wanted to embrace him. When they married, he didn't know what happened to her. If she hadn't been so scared, if she'd trusted his love, things could've been so different. She shook herself. That was the past. They found each other again. They'd live their love in the light, God's light.

Barrington unfolded his arms, then tapped his index finger against his lips. "Why isn't your daughter here to accuse him directly?"

Pulling his hands to his face, Mr. Calloway sounded

like lightning had stricken him. "She's locked in Bedlam! A danger to herself."

Barrington moved closer to the witness and raised his hand on the rail. "I know you are in pain. But, the description of the man your daughter described." His voice slowed, each syllable pierced her heart. Maybe the hearts of all who heard. "Sir, the thing that haunts her to this day, was it a ragged thin man or a thick horrid beast?"

Mr. Calloway looked up and turned his head to the prisoner's box. "A beast."

The crowd gasped.

Barrington had done it, gotten the man to see past his anger.

Pride swelled in her heart.

Her husband retook his seat at the barristers' table.

Mr. Hessing stood back up. "Can you trust a description from the girl? Her mind is besought with struggles."

"That would be the same as not believing her account at all." Barrington leaned forward in his chair. "Pardon, my lord justice."

The smirk on her husband's face didn't look as if he was sorry.

Justice Burns shook his head. "Proceed, Mr. Hessing."

Sarah's father leaned forward. "She told the truth. I believe her."

A grimace painted the prosecutor's face. "I'm done with this witness."

"My daughter didn't lie." Mr. Calloway stepped down from the box and stomped all the way out of the courtroom.

Mr. Hessing picked up a piece a paper then turned

towards the gallery. "I call Mr. Joseph Tantlin."

Samuel squeezed Amora's hand. "Buck up, Amora. If Mr. Norton sees you flustered, the man will throttle everyone within reach."

"I will. I can't disappoint him when it's my turn."

After dispensing Tantlin's testimony as hearsay, Barrington plodded over to Miller and made his voice a whisper. "Ask the judge to release you. They've charged the wrong man."

His friend looked down at him, squinting.

"Just do it."

"Mr. Justice, sir." Miller's words sounded squeaky. "They've charged...the wrong man. Release...me?"

The crowd roared with laughter.

"My lord, what my client is saying is that all the evidence which supported his indictment is hearsay. None of the witnesses can say conclusively that Miller abducted them let alone any of the other atrocities."

Mr. Hessing leapt to his feet. "The nature of the crimes is so despicable. The Abductor has been shrewd in selecting his victims. I--"

"I'd like to call a witness to attest that Miller could not have done this." Barrington looked into the crowd and caught Amora's stare. Nothing under the sun would make him compel his wife to the stand. "I request Miss Cynthia Miller."

Burns nodded. "Alright, bring her to the stand."

Hessing retook his seat, grimacing at Barrington.

Cynthia descended the stairs and slipped into the stand. The men in the crowd seemed to lean forward with bulging eyes, surely to ogle the viper. One clapped as if she were performing at the theatre. It was a good thing her character didn't shine through her tight gown.

With a shake of his noggin, Barrington approached. "Miss Miller, please tell the court about your brother, Gerald Miller."

"He's the kindest of men. When our father died, he took care of me and our poor mother." She gripped the rail and looked toward the jurymen. "He's the one who encouraged me to sing."

Her lips drew into a pout. Lyrics of a hymn passed out of that lying mouth. "I once was lost." Her voice continued for several stanzas.

Grace was amazing, even repeated by a forked tongue.

The judge, like almost every other fellow in the court, pressed his head closer.

Her angelic tune reverberated off the burnished paneling, and the prisoner board, making a sweet echo.

Yet, knowing the truth of this woman, Barrington's throat constricted from her sour notes. His ears burned. A smart barrister, a loyal husband should never have fallen prey to the singer's smiles. Such anguish his thoughtlessness caused Amora.

As Cynthia continued singing, Barrington again inspected the jurymen. Grins went up everywhere. Was this display enough to erase the ugliness of the charges?

He unfolded his stiff hands, easing them to his side. He couldn't let anyone see his disgust. "It is a warm picture you paint of Gerald Miller, a fine protector and mentor. Miss Miller, do you believe your brother capable of such evil?"

She gripped the dock as if to steady herself from a faint. "A thousand times no. He is the kindest, gentlest soul."

Barrington sat back at the barrister's bench. At least

the woman's duplicity wasn't exposed.

Hessing trudged to the witness box. Even his face seemed light. Was he also smitten by the woman? "Miss Miller, you seem so sweet. Indeed, the love of a brother is so touching. Is that why you hid the deserter?"

"I'm sorry." Cynthia's mouth dropped open. "I don't understand."

"Did Gerald Miller not leave his service early?"

She pulled out her fan and waved it. "Yes, but he was wounded and confused."

Hessing tugged his hands behind his back and faced the crowd. "So this paragon deserted? He let down Mother England in her time of need. Why wouldn't he have at her daughters, too?"

"That's a lie." Cynthia shifted and gazed at the jurymen. "Gerald came home to protect us, to aid us in our time of woe." She started crying. "Would you let your family fall to ruin? No, sir. No good man would."

The males in the gallery nodded their heads. Cynthia was good for something.

His mentor spun with a lightness of foot and approached the weeping singer. "I suppose that is why you hid him when he was found with the dead woman?"

Stopping in the middle of her jig, Cynthia beat upon the rail. "Gerald didn't kill Miss Druby!"

Barrington dropped his head into his hand. The woman just left an opening for his nearly defeated opponent.

"You admit that Gerald was found with the dead woman, Miss Druby?" Hessing moved closer to the stand. He drew himself up as if to use his girth to separate Cynthia from the audience.

"He didn't kill her. The Abductor did."

"You say that with such assurance. I submit you know who the Abductor is."

Cynthia reached into her reticule and gripped something. "I know Gerald is not guilty." As she craned her neck toward the gallery, her face became blank. She put her hand down at her side.

The button. At the first opportunity, Barrington would snatch it from her palm.

Hessing turned to Justice Burns. "Since this case now hinges upon proving that Gerald Miller is Hampshire's murderer, I will now call witnesses to prove it."

His mentor's smirk said everything, chilling the marrow in Barrington's limbs. Amora would soon be called to testify. The Old Bailey, the law he loved would destroy everything he held dear.

Chapter Eight: The Truth Shall Reign

Barrington shook his head. There was no way to lessen the damage of Mr. Johansson's testimony of finding Gerald with Nan Druby.

Gerald looked to the floor. The pain on his face, the pinch of his lips was intense. Hearing Mr. Johansson announce to the world how he discovered Miss Druby's lifeless body, strangled at Gerald's feet had to be devastating.

From the near silence in the courtroom, it had surely sucked away all the ground Barrington had made with the earlier testimony. "Did Mrs. Druby seem beaten?"

Johansson rocked back and forth, his low heels clicked with each sway. "No, she didn't have a speck on her. She might not have fought with Miller. It's hard to say."

"Gerald Miller is the type of man who would step forward and take a bullet meant to kill you." Barrington slowed his pitch, lowered his shaking fists. "Based on your description of the wound gushing from Miller's head and not a spot of blood on Miss Druby, isn't it more likely Miller was hit and incapacitated by the

Abductor? With Miller unable to help, the brute strangled Miss Druby."

Johansson nodded over his jiggling belly. "Could be. Hard to say."

This man was no help. Barrington went back to his chair. He glimpsed at Miller. *Please say something to show your innocence.*

His friend looked hopeless. All the air in his chest must have leaked out, leaving him flat and lifeless. Would the jurymen see it as reverie or guilt?

Defeated, Barrington took his seat.

Hessing smiled big as if he'd eaten every teacake in a sweet shop. "I've a final witness. I call Mrs. Amora Norton, formerly Miss Amora Tomàs. Her testimony will be conclusive."

Barrington's heart sunk as he focused on his wife coming down from the gallery.

Mrs. Tomàs and the vicar steadied her until she reached the bottom of the steps. Wilson patted her arm and looked down upon her as if to bolster her.

Part grateful, part jealous, Barrington wiped his brow and watched Amora float across the floor and climb into the witness box. Like a butter colored flower, her cheeks matched the color of her sunny gold dress. She looked good, seemed well, but could she endure the forthcoming storm?

His heart lurched. She seemed so tiny, so vulnerable within the frame of the stand. Why couldn't he protect her from this?

The judge shifted in his chair. "Mr. Norton, were you aware--"

Barrington straightened within his chair. "Yes, my lord."

Hessing kissed Amora's hand. "I discovered, from the administer of Bedlam, her connections to Sarah Calloway. They both were taken and held together by Miller."

The crowd roared. "Hang 'em! Hang 'em!"

His mentor smiled even wider, savoring this opportunity to serve Barrington comeuppance on a platter. "Mrs. Norton, you've come to this court today to shed light on this miserable business. I know it is difficult, but can you tell the court about the evening when Miss Druby died?"

She clutched the railing, fingers shaking. "I was trapped in the Priory as was Miss Druby. Sarah had already been released. The monster got rid of the women he abused."

The crowd silenced. Amora's small tone seemed to have squeezed the air out of everyone in the court.

Hessing started pacing in front of the witness box. "So you are a victim of the Abductor?"

With a raise of her countenance, she released a slow breath. "Yes."

Again, the absence of noise in the Old Bailey made Barrington's pulse rise.

"I was abducted by the villain on 13 April, 1814 whilst I painted in my father's orchards very close to the Norman relic in Clanville, the Priory. Yes, April 13."

Hessing guffawed and stopped in his tracks. "How can you be so certain?"

Her gaze seemed to focus on Barrington for a moment. He hoped he didn't look like an ogre sitting on his hands.

"It was exactly a fortnight since my father's passing." She smoothed her fingers along the rail. "I count things.

It helps me focus." She folded her arms. "As I painted a watercolor of the Priory outside of the village of Clanville in Hampshire, someone grabbed me from behind. He struck me as I fought. I awakened in the dark root cellar of the Priory."

"You fought? You were taken without consent?"

"Yes." Her gaze lowered. "I never consented, ever."

Posting between Barrington and the witness box, Hessing lowered his voice. "There's no easy way to say this. Were you tampered with?"

"He punched me." Her tone decelerated. "He kept me against my will." Her hands shook. "Almost two months."

The lack of surety in her tone was palatable. It didn't matter. Barrington would love her no matter what. Did she know that?

Turning, Hessing's face wore a frown. He wasn't unfeeling, just a man set on winning. He tugged at his wig. "Could you recognize him, the Abductor?"

"No."

Hessing looked disturbed, furrowing his brow. "But in your sworn testimony..."

Amora nodded. In clear loud tones, she stated, "I said that I could identify that Mr. Miller was in the Priory, and he was. He was rescuing Mrs. Druby."

The crowds squealed.

Hessing marched to the barrister's table, planting himself right in front of Barrington. "This is some joke, set up by your husband."

"No." She pulled from her reticule several pieces of papers. "Here are the accounts of four doctors and Mrs. Henutsen Tomàs's statement attesting to my abduction and condition upon escaping. I was there, Mr. Hessing.

And I know that Mr. Miller is innocent."

Hessing stumbled back to his seat.

Barrington stood and took the documents from her shaking fingers, giving them to Judge Burns. "Amora...Mrs. Norton, please state exactly what happened." He swallowed hard. "Spare no detail for the court."

Her husband looked at Amora with such tenderness, yet a lump still formed in her throat. It was time to say the truth to the world.

A smile formed on his lips, then thinned. "Please tell me, the court what happened."

She swallowed and scanned the packed courtroom. Everyone must be here. So many faces. Cynthia sat in the front row sobbing into a handkerchief. Samuel's dark mop of hair bowed in prayer. Mama held his hand and nodded as if giving her permission.

Lord Charleton, along with his brother, the reclusive Lord Hampshire stood at opposite ends of the high gallery. Even the Duchess of Hampshire attended.

The babe quickened in her stomach. She patted him. *God, don't let my courage diminish.*

Barrington's jaw trembled. He craned his neck toward the ceiling beams. "Mrs. Norton, I know this is difficult, but tell the court what you remember. You haven't come this far on your journey to stop now. I trust...I trust that everyone wants to hear your story."

Her husband trusted her and encouraged her. She almost raised a hand to his dear face. Instead, she clasped the wooden railing. "A shout bellowed through the Priory. I knew it wasn't the Abductor. The evil man never spoke above a whisper. The footsteps moved closer to my chained cell, and I heard clearly Gerald Miller's voice."

"Ma'am, what did he say?"

She licked her dry lips. "He asked, 'Is anyone in here?'"

Pacing to stand closer to the prisoner's stand, Barrington's tall form seemed very stiff in his movement. With a blank face, he locked his gaze with hers. "Did you answer?"

"I was afraid at first. My mouth felt parched, as if it were packed with cotton. I hadn't had anything to drink that day, but I did answer."

A growl uttered from Barrington's mouth. He rubbed his jaw until it held no expression again. "What did Miller do?"

"He recognized my voice and told me not to worry. He tried to open the door but couldn't get the chain off. I still hear the heavy clanging of the chains. He tried several times but he couldn't get them removed. I still hear the clang, clang of the chains. They were so heavy, unbreakable..."

Of its own volition, her voice trailed off. A tremor set in her fingers, and she started counting planks on the floor.

"Continue, Mrs. Norton, with your testimony." Barrington shuttled closer. "Please."

"I told him the Abductor would return soon and to go save Miss Druby. I heard horses' hooves as the light began to disappear."

"Mrs. Norton. You've said enough. We can infer--"

Hessing stood up. "No. She must state her testimony." He wrenched the back of his neck. "No matter how horrible."

Justice Burns grimaced, but nodded. "Please continue, Mrs. Norton."

She dug into reticule for one of her notes of encouragement, but couldn't finger any, just Barrington's button. It didn't jingle like the buttons of what freed her. She raised her head as more memories returned. "I shouted to Mr. Miller to hurry. The Abductor had arrived. He always arrived when it grew dark." Tears leaked, but she didn't swipe at them. She would let the world see the stains. No more hiding.

Tugging off his wig, Barrington came near, put a finger to her cheek and caught a few of the drops. "Did Miller leave you as you advised?"

"Yes, he promised to tell you...where I was held. Mr. Miller went to save Miss Druby. Then I heard drumming boot heels, the heavy footfalls of the monster."

He stepped back and moved closer to the jury stand. "What occurred next?"

Sounds of captivity returned, echoing within her skull. Her breath came in gasps. "I heard yelling! Lots of yelling."

"How many voices?"

Forcing air into her lungs, Amora looked up to the gallery and then to the roof of the Old Bailey. "Three. I heard Gerald Miller's, Miss Druby's, and the Abductor's. Then screaming." An ache ripped through her temples. The memories chiseled away at her composure. She panted and clutched the rail to stay upright. "Endless screaming, worse than ever."

Barrington's mouth moved, but she heard nothing. She pulled her hands to her ears.

His lips formed the words, "God give her strength."

She had to finish this, intact, with her wits. It was the

only way to save Gerald and reclaim the bits of her soul the true abductor took. She blinked until the pain in her temples subsided.

Barrington's voice became clear. "Can you continue?"

She nodded. "I heard the chains fall to the floor. The torturer came. He...he shouted at me, said I caused him to do this. Then he struck me with his heavy hand. I don't remember any more."

Barrington folded his arms. With his eyes closed, he looked as if he'd rip the walls down. "Mrs. Norton, you've remembered enough." With a lift of his lids, he unveiled raw anger stricken pupils. "You are so brave."

He sucked in a breath, before reaching back and tugging his wig on lopsided. "Tell the good jurymen if Mr. Miller is the Abductor."

Each of the fellows seemed frozen as if posed for a portrait for her to paint. Tall, short, fat and skinny, all sat quietly on the edge of their seats, waiting. She leaned in their direction. "No, Mr. Miller is not him!"

Murmurs swept the length of the courtroom. Not a one yelled, *Hang 'em*.

Barrington turned to Justice Burns. "By the logic brought by the prosecution if Gerald Miller is not the Abductor then he did not abduct Miss Calloway and Mrs. Tantlin. My client is not the guilty party."

His head dipped toward Miller, as if to send a signal.

Mr. Miller banged the frame of his stand. "Judge, I'm...innocent. Please re...lease me." He waved at her. "Thank you, ma'am."

Justice Burns rotated to Mr. Hessing. "Do you have anything more to ask of this brave witness?"

Mr. Hessing shook his head. "I'm finished."

The judge pivoted to the jury. "You must now decide

based on the evidence you've heard if you believe Mr. Gerald Miller is guilty of abducting Miss Sarah Calloway and Mrs. Anna Tantlin. Norton, take a moment and escort your wife from the witness box."

"My lord, I'll do just that." Barrington held an arm up to Amora.

She clasped it. The joining of their palms, the strength of his fingers entwining with his. If only the jurymen would pronounce Gerald innocent.

Seeing Cynthia's reticule tottering on the rail, Barrington remembered the hidden clue. He steered his beautiful wife to a seat near the viper.

Cynthia's brow rose as she sat on her palms, her pouty lips poked out. The noise of the crowd fell upon his shoulders, but he kept his gaze on her satin reticule. With a slight of hand, he knocked it off the rail, dumping its contents to the floor.

The button she'd kept all these years rolled to his foot. He picked up the silver thing. Eyes growing larger than silver dollars, he identified the crest.

Cynthia frowned so deeply her chin disappeared.

Barrington didn't care. He pushed his thumb over the crest as he put the button in his pocket. His fingers throbbed, aching to kill. He knew the identity of the blackguard. Leaning close to Amora's ear, he whispered, "This will be over soon. Love you."

Turning, he allowed the smile he donned for his wife to disappear. As soon as Miller was proclaimed innocent, Barrington would send runners to arrest the true Dark Walk Abductor.

Justice Burns pounded his fist. All conversation stopped. Every head in the crowd pointed toward his desk. "Jurymen, what say ye?"

Every mouth quieted. All ears were craned toward the men sitting in judgment, the deciders of Miller's fate.

The lead man jumped from his chair. "We find the defendant not guilty."

The gallery roared with chants. "Not guilty! Not guilty!"

Barrington's heart started to thump. Some overly exuberant person might bump into his petite wife. Where was she? He squinted but excited spectators bounced up and down, obscuring his view.

Justice Burns knocked along his table. His palm looked blackened from the effort. His bailiff offered him a deep-brown gavel, which Burns seized. He pounded the surface again. "Mr. Miller, you have been found innocent of the two charges of abduction and assault, but you will be held in Newgate and then transported from there to stand trial in the assize in Winchester for the Hampshire charges. The case will be taken with the September circuit. Bailiff."

The crowd went wild, shrieking. Joyful and loud, so different from the hanging mob of before. They surrounded the prisoner dock and the bar.

Barrington pushed his way through and stalked over to Miller. "The assize meets in September. One hundred and twenty days and you'll be free. You've slept longer."

"Thank you." With a tight, bony grip, Miller seized Barrington's hand. "Tell the Mrs., grateful." Chin high, his friend stepped down, plodding between the gaoler and the bailiff.

Barrington pivoted and fought his way through the well-wishers and the pats on the back, heading toward Amora's seat.

Beakes planted in front of him. "Congratulations. I did as I said. My men are at every door looking to stop trouble. I hope we have no hard feelings." He stuck out a hand.

Barrington clasped it. No one could procure runners faster than this solicitor. "Get your men ready." As soon as I attend to my wife, we will go get the true Abductor. You'll have your big catch."

The man nodded then disappeared into the milling crowd.

A few more steps and Barrington was stopped again as Hessing laid a palm on his shoulder. "You beat me, Norton. I suppose you are better at the law."

Barrington hesitated then pivoted, standing toe-to-toe with his mentor in front of the barristers' bar. "On the contrary, if you hadn't brought my wife into this, I would've lost."

"A wins a win." Hessing took off his wig, left it on the table, and plodded out of the courtroom.

Barrington touched the cast-off. He'd defeated his mentor, the person who engendered the power of the court. A sigh filled his lungs. This was a great way to end his legal career. This trial would be Barrington's last in the Old Bailey. A quiet home with Amora and their child, that was his heart's desire.

And the Abductor's head was on a stake. Maybe a bullet between the eyes. Barrington dumped his court wig atop Hessing's, then marched to Amora's seat.

It was empty.

Only a pouting Cynthia remained.

He scanned the chamber. Almost everyone had left, but the noise from the hall was deafening.

His wife must be with her mother and the vicar.

Hopefully, no newsmen hovered about her, harassing her. She'd been through enough today.

"Mr. Norton." Cynthia's voice could pierce the walls. "Why couldn't you get my brother freed?"

"He will be. Things have to run their course, but you could have ended this, years ago." He held up the crested button, displaying the tarnished family coat of arms. "Why?"

"I'm so sorry." She doubled over into a heap of satin, a crying puddle of lies, shaking and sobbing on the floor.

"Evil woman." He returned the proof to his pocket.

"Don't hate me, Barrington. Please don't." Her wailing increased as he plodded away. "I did it for Gerald. It provided the laudanum to ease his pain."

"There is always an excuse. Isn't there?" He started to the door. "Maybe, you should be implicated in this."

"Yes, she knew." A man popped up from a seat in the high gallery and started down the steps. "She has been demanding payments and favors for years."

Blood rushed Barrington's eyes. He charged at the man, pinning the villain against the wall. The man's head bobbled against the plaster. "I was beginning to think you a decent man." Barrington pushed his forearm deep into the ogre's throat. "How could you have done this? Hurt Amora and the others."

The man flayed his arms, but no power on earth could stop Barrington's death grip.

"Not him!" Cynthia yelled between cries. "His brother. His brother's the Dark Walk Abductor."

"What? The earl?" Barrington raised his hands. "Your brother, Lord Clanville is the fiend?"

Charleton slid to the floor rubbing his neck. He loosed his wilted cravat, jingling the large buttons on his waistcoat.

Is that why Amora loved noisy buttons? Could it be her remembering Charleton leading her to freedom?

"I've been covering his scandals for years. I can't do it anymore. Norton, believe me. When I found out, I stopped him from hurting anyone else. I was the one who unchained the root cellar door. I waited and watched until Miss Tomàs crawled out and made it back to Tomàs Manor."

Was it true? Hot air squeezed from Barrington's lungs. No time for proof. "Where's your brother? Tobias Charleton, the Earl of Clanville. Where is Clanville now?"

Chapter Nine: For Her

Amora took a deep breath. The crowds pushed her, sweeping her along like fast-moving river water. One portly man nearly stomped on her toes. She kept stepping backward, until her slippers stood on the floorboards of the hall.

"Good afternoon, Mrs. Norton." The words were light, barely above a whisper.

She rotated. Instead of seeing the handsome face of Samuel or Barrington, the Earl of Clanville's scarred countenance greeted her.

He dipped his onyx top hat. "This way to get away from the crowd."

Not waiting for her response, he lightly tugged her forearm.

She pulled free, averting her gaze to the burnished paneling along the walls. "I need no assistance. I'm waiting for my husband, my lord."

"The papermen will want a statement." His voice was low, raspy. "You can hide in here."

Something in his soft tone chilled her, prickling her

arms. She took a few paces away from him. "No, thank you. My party will be here shortly."

A man bumped against her, knocking her against the wall next to the Duchess of Cheshire. The tall man shrugged. "Sorry, miss." He nodded and kept moving toward the door.

The duchess gripped Amora's hand. "You are so brave, Mrs. Norton."

The earl moved toward them. His boots made a familiar rhythm. "It's not safe here."

Her heart raced. She gripped her wrists trying to remember she was in the light, in a crowded hall. Nothing to fear. "I'm going back into the courtroom. Good day."

The duchess squinted and stayed at her side. "I'll wait with you. My husband went to congratulate Mr. Norton."

She turned and adjusted her bonnet letting air cool her fevered brow.

The pounding of his heels against the hardwoods vibrated her spine. "But I want another moment, pet...to offer my compliments."

Thump. Thump. Boot heels. Bricks falling. Another memory of a hard slap to her cheek surfaced.

"All are in your debt." He clasped her elbow.

Even before he touched her, she knew. With all her strength, she pivoted and slugged him. Again and again, she struck him.

"Mrs. Norton—"

He grabbed the duchess by the mouth, covered her within his cape drawing her close, shielding her resistance from the passerby. "Yell, and I'll hurt her badly."

Amora struck at his arm and made her tone a whisper. "Let her go. It's me you've wanted."

She looked right and left. The crowd just milled about, not noticing.

The duchess clawed at the hands blocking her windpipe.

Not wanting another to suffer, she nodded to the monster. "Release her and I will..." The words died on her tongue. She would never consent to the monster.

He did as she directed, releasing Lady Cheshire's throat but kept his arm about her middle pushing her into an open room. Then he reached for Amora and flung her inside, too.

She clasped a table edge to regain her balance. The small chamber held only a table, a chair and a large window. There was no way out.

His large body blocked the entrance, the only means of escape. He let go of Lady Cheshire. She dropped to the floor.

Her spectacles spun as they hit the floor. "Why have you done this?"

"He's the Monster. He's the one who abducted me and the others."

"Yes." His tone was low, menacing. "And we have unfinished business."

Light from the leaded panes covered her. Fear and air fought within her lungs, making it difficult for her nostrils to work. She should turn and beat upon the window, but couldn't risk placing her back to the earl. That was how he'd taken her before, how he tried to take her again. "The Earl of Clanville is the monster, and you'll take no more from me."

The duchess kicked and moved from his grasp,

scrambling to Amora's side. "That thing is the Abductor of the ton. How? Why?"

He rubbed his scarred jaw. "A carriage fire took my face. Darkness makes the sneers go away."

Amora reached down and grabbed Lady Cheshire's hand helping her to stand. "Don't turn your back. Make him show his cowardly face here in the light."

The young woman linked arms with Amora just as Sarah would. "Weren't you were raised to be a gentleman, not a criminal?"

His lips lifted into a half-smile, the unburnt side cooperating. "Only my pet sees a difference."

Pulse racing, Amora shifted when the monster took a step. "You abused and you killed. How can you live with that?"

A low rumble of chortles bubbled as he gripped the table. "They don't mock me anymore. Neither will your friend, when it's her turn."

Amora dragged the duchess backward. She couldn't know how vicious the earl was. The thick moulding of the window's ledge pressed into her spine. "I'll scream if you come any closer."

He tugged a knife from his waistband. "Come with me now, my pet, and I won't hurt this one."

"My mama, my husband, my friends. They will see I'm missing. This time we will be rescued."

Eyeing the door, Amora estimated that at least one of the women could make it. She pulled the duchess past her and swung her reticule at the monster.

Bumping into the table but bouncing in the right direction, the young lady made it to the door and slid out of the room.

In a blink, he clutched her bag within his leather-clad

palms. "You were always the most clever. Consent now. With you, I will be complete."

The door burst open as Vicar Wilson pressed inside. "Get away from Mrs. Norton."

The duchess must have alerted him.

Her heart lifted.

But the earl spun and thrust his dagger into the vicar.

With a thud, the knife sunk into Samuel's chest. He doubled over and fell to the floor.

Amora's heart leaked as if it too was stabbed. Her friend could be dying from the monster. She slipped past Lord Clanville and leapt upon Samuel. Her friend had to be well. He had to. She pulled at the blade but couldn't make it move. Gathering her shawl, she pressed it against the wound. That would stymie the bleeding. "Be fine."

The earl hovered. His shadow smothered her, surrounding her with memories of the Priory. "Come and I'll send someone to help your friend. Consent."

Samuel stroked her chin. He mouthed, "No." Then his lids shut.

She couldn't remember how to breathe. Thinking of Barrington's song made the air go in and out. "Barrington! Help!"

The monster put a hand to her lips. "Quiet."

Tears flooded her face, but she put her full weight on Samuel's wound. Her shawl colored scarlet. "I won't go with you. And you'll not escape this time."

He shoved a chair under the knob. "No, this time you will consent. "

Barrington had barely finished giving Beakes instructions when his frantic mother-in-law held up by James burst into the courtroom.

Mrs. Tomàs traipsed faster, charging straight toward the barrister's bar. He caught the woman in his arms.

"Amora is missing. The vicar and I have been looking. James says that she hasn't left the Old Bailey." The woman trembled. She looked ashen. "Where is she?"

"Tis true, sir." James took off his tricorn with shaking fingers. "I've been with the carriages. She hasn't come that way. The runners are on the doors."

"My daughter can't be gone." Mrs. Tomàs started to cry. "This can't happen again. Don't let it."

"My brother." Charleton paled. "He may have come. I didn't see him, but he might have been in the crowd."

Barrington turned to the suddenly composed Cynthia. She wiped her dripping nose on a handkerchief. "I saw him. He was here. I don't know where he went."

Lord Clanville might have Amora? Barrington's pulse exploded. His heart felt as if it had been ripped from his chest. "You waited until now to mention it. There is no redemption for you. Charleton, Beakes, get the runners. We must search until we find her."

Lady Cheshire broke open the barrister's door to the courtroom. "Mr. Norton! He's got her in a room. Someone has to help her."

Like a bullet, Barrington shot into the hall. James followed close on his heels as they checked empty room after empty room.

Though the crowds had thinned, Amora nor the earl could be found.

Barrington's heart thundered. All he could do was pray. They came to the last door. A faint voice echoed through the wood.

"Barrington!"

He slammed his shoulder against the frame, pushing

until there was a crack.

"Amora!"

Barrington's baritone voice fluttered her heart. Her breathing came in gasps. He'd come to save her.

She opened her mouth to scream.

Clanville yanked the knife from Samuel and lifted her. He pressed the point of the blade to her neck. His hold, the same as when he grabbed her years ago, was harsh. Her skin chafed beneath the rough feel of his leather gloves.

Though her voice abandoned her, she elbowed and kicked to no avail. His arm was too firm. His fingers clawed her like a falcon's talons. As her vision started to dim, a pain shot through her abdomen. Her heart sank to her child, wrapping about it, trying hard to protect it. "Barrington!"

"I should've known you wouldn't consent. At the Priory, I did everything to break your spirit, but couldn't."

Her eyes opened wide. She hadn't given up then. She couldn't give up now.

The gap in the door expanded. Barrington snaked through with James at his side. "Clanville, release her."

James jumped to Samuel, fished off the man's cravat and covered the wound.

Barrington powered closer. "Let her go."

Chuckling, Clanville squeezed her neck. "No, Barrister. Court is done. Be gone."

Barrington's face looked of stone. He stripped off his court silks, and stepped into Clanville's shadow. "The crown's court is done, but not mine. You will die for all the evil you have done. I am your judge, jury, and executioner."

That hurting heart of hers started climbing. Barrington would save her. God hadn't abandoned them. Maybe there was still a chance. Hope filled her lungs. She beat at the earl's arm and claimed a deep breath.

Barrington waved his fists in the air. "I'm not asking again."

"Barrister, there's no stopping me." The monster stroked a strand of her hair, wrapping it about his finger, touching it to his burnt lips. "I should've finished you in the alley before the duke came. I can't leave without her. I've waited too long *for her*. All *for her*."

"Never." Barrington stepped closer. She could almost touch him. "Surrender now or die here. I will kill you."

The earl backed up against the window, dragging her, crushing her neck with his forearm. "Pet, you're not free. I'll kill the barrister and anyone else keeping you from me."

Amora closed her eyes as she doubled over. "No. Don't hurt another. Let this be over. I can't bear anymore."

"Don't stop fighting, Amora. Tobias Charleton, I won't stop until your skull caves in, worse than you did to Miller."

His grip on her shoulder shifted. The knife cut on her neck, dripping dark drops onto her bodice. "Then maybe she and I will die together."

Noise from outside filtered through the lead glass. The courtyard and street were filled with people.

"Let her go. It's over, Clanville. You've been exposed."

The earl moved the knife from her throat, as he peered through the glass. "A crowd gathers."

He raised a hand as if to strike her. "You kept yelling. You did this, Pet."

She squinted, preparing for the blow.

Barrington blunted the monster's arm in mid swing and absorbed a punch to the back as he pulled Amora to the floor.

She saw a blade reflected in the earl's eyes. "The knife, Barrington!"

Her husband spun and wrestled Clanville's grip on the dagger.

Her insides burned, but she couldn't move.

Barrington knocked the blade away and pounded Clanville's face and gut with a flurry of punches. His hands closed about Hampshire's windpipe. "Guilty. The sentence is death."

"Sir!" James's panicked voice. "Throw him through the window!"

Barrington turned to the courtyard.

In synchronization with the muzzle's flash, he shoved Hampshire against the window then dropped, shielding Amora.

The glass shattered as a boom filled the air. Clanville fell next to them as shards rained all about them.

Barrington stood. Amora caught sight of the earl's back. Smoke billowed from a smoldering bullet hole. Was the nightmare over?

Barrington pivoted and shook diamond like fragments from his coat. His thick hair glittered with light. "Can you hear me?"

He pulled her face into his hands.

She couldn't respond, the pain in her body siphoned all her air.

"Amora, you're free now. I'll take care of you."

The joy of being freed from the monster disappeared. Her babe, she was losing him. Maybe this time she'd go too. "I'll be with our children, Barrington."

He gathered her in his arms. "Don't go. Fight."

"I'll give them a Holy kiss. God and Papa, we'll take care of them."

She closed her eyes and for the first time welcomed the darkness.

Chapter Ten: The Balance of Life

Barrington paced back and forth in the parlor. Neither Hudson or Mrs. Tomàs had come down from Amora's bedchamber. They banned him for asking too many questions and getting in the way. James pulled him from the room when they said they'd send for him if Amora grew worse.

Lord Cheshire also paced as his duchess sat on the sofa with hands folded in prayer. They'd insisted upon waiting with him and Barrington gained comfort from the company.

Cheshire stopped in front of his wife. "You said it was dangerous for me to be immersed in politics, Gaia. It seems you court danger too, in a court no less."

He took her hand and kissed it. "What would Mary and I do without you?"

She smiled up at him with a look of complete soul connection. "I hope you and Mary and our child to come never have to know."

"You're...? We're going to...?"

"Yes, William. My abigail confirmed the days for me

this morning."

The duke blinked heavily and drew her head against his waist. "God is good."

Barrington watched their joy and felt happiness for them. He and Amora were that happy last night. They had regained each other's trust. They had to be that happy again. "Duke, you should take your wife home. I'll send word of Amora's condition."

"We'll wait a little longer. Mrs. Norton saved my wife and our joy to come." He dimpled saying the words. "It's the least we can do."

The duchess patted the cushion next to her. "Sit, William. We must know about Vicar Wilson, too. I sent him into that room. We must know how he fares."

Heavy footfalls sounded on the stairs.

Everyone swiveled their heads to see what the news would be.

Hudson soon appeared at the parlor entrance. "The vicar lost a great deal of blood, but he will live as long as infection doesn't set in."

Barrington rushed to his cousin. "And Amora?"

His cousin's face hadn't changed from blank. "It's still too soon to tell. She's comfortable. Her vitals are weak. The babe is not as active as he was before. I just don't know."

Enough of waiting for word, he nodded at his cousin and headed for the stairs. "Duke, take your wife home. Oh, and the ship you wanted me to locate was the Blessing. It left Liverpool about that timeframe with cargo to Africa. One ship manifest marked Xhosa sailed to Jamaica."

The duke stood and put his wife's palm upon his arm.

They looked at each other, with love and something

else, just as thick and powerful. Empathy, maybe forgiveness of the past.

"Thank you, Norton. I needed the confirmation of where my wife's father may have been enslaved. This is good to know, but I think I will focus on the future."

"The future," the duchess said as she yawned. "Send word as soon as Mrs. Norton is better. She will get better."

Barrington nodded and as politely as he could, turned and flew up the treads. He pushed inside Amora's chamber.

She was very pale lying in her bed.

Mrs. Tomàs looked weepy and broken sitting by her daughter's side. "If I'd known that it was the Earl of Clanville who did this to her, I would've shot him five years ago. He sat at my table. Ate my pies. All the time a villain."

Plodding close to the woman, he put his hand on her shoulder. "Well, shooting him now will be without charges. I talked to the magistrate. No one blames you for taking the runner's flintlock and shooting. I'm just glad you are a great shot. Go check on the vicar and then get a little sleep. I'll send for you if anything changes."

"I can't move from her. I won't."

Barrington wrenched at his neck. "But you sent me from the room?"

Her brow raised as she cocked her head toward him. "Brooding is helping?"

"I suppose it's not." He plodded to his side of the bed and sat next to Amora. He fingered her temples. "She's beautiful even when she sleeps."

He stretched and reached for her pouch of notes. "If

you can hear me, Amora, I think I'll read to you. For you are more than a conqueror. You are brilliant, and brave and free."

Each piece of foolscap, he unfolded and refolded until he'd gone through the pile. Then he just watched her breathing and waited for another miracle. The girl who survived the monster couldn't disappear.

He wasn't above begging God for another moment to hear Amora's laughter or to see her eyes light with a smile. The love of his life couldn't be gone.

Amora opened one lid, then the other. Candles, many shapes and sizes, dripped wax from the sconces scattered about the room. Their glow reflected on the crisp white sheets. She wasn't at the Priory or any dark cell. A long sigh left her mouth. She'd awakened in her bedchamber at Mayfair. How?

Too tired to figure things out, she soaked up the light and smoothed her stiff fingers on the cool bedclothes, the fluffy pillow on her stomach. The soft starchy smell of freshly laundered linens wrapped around her, comforting her bruised body.

Mrs. Gretling must've cleaned things. Such a good woman.

Not wanting to dwell on the emptiness in her heart, she moved her thumbs from the pillow. Maybe if she closed her eyes, she could pretend this was just another horrid dream. But it felt true.

Tears leaked out of her eyes, though she was too stiff to swipe at them. The Lord gives and takes away.

An ache coursed the length of her legs and arms, ending at her heart. She stopped attempting to rise and laid still.

Her head was light, but a vague memory of drinking fouled tea remained. Like a flash of lightning, another image took its place, the vision of Lord Clanville falling onto the floor. Was her monster dead?

Not wanting to think of her abductor, of all he'd cost her, she pinched her eyes shut. Yet, the feeling of loss wouldn't go away. How would she and Barrington get on now? She'd failed this baby, too. "I'm sorry."

A low snore filtered in her ear.

She turned her hurting neck and spied Barrington sleeping in a Klismos chair, one from his study. His tailcoat hung in disarray, twisted and wrinkled on the chair back as if he'd just cast it aside.

His head bobbled to a steady rhythm. He looked tired, with deep shadows beneath his eyes. The moonlight from the open window highlighted the silver threads in his dark hair. She counted more there than ever before.

God knew best, even when bad things happened.

Mouth dry, she strained and reached for a water goblet seated on the bed table.

With clumsy movements, her fingertips made a tinkling sound on the glass rim.

Alerted, Barrington stood to attention. His fists were drawn as if he were ready to pounce on anything or anyone amiss. "Amora! You're awake."

He took the cup from her hand and moved it to her lips.

A few sips of the precious liquid wet her tongue. Beads of moisture fell into her parched throat. With a final swallow, she patted the glass for him to raise it.

Barrington settled it, then gazed at her. With his index finger, he stroked her chin.

What could she say to him? He must be so grieved.

"How do you feel, Amora?"

She stared at him and batted wet eyes. Barrington knew this would happen.

A frown swallowed his smile. "Are you distressed? In any pain?"

"Forgive me, Barrington." Cries from her heart wrenched out of her mouth.

With great care, he gathered her into his arms. Easing onto the mattress, he rocked her. "Sweetheart, I need you to calm."

How could he be so kind? They'd lost another babe. Surely, his shirtsleeves would drip like a leaking pail from her ragged tears. "Forgive me."

"For what? For being the bravest girl in the world."

He fluffed a pillow and slipped it against the headboard. Smoothing her back, he pinned her against his warm chest. "It's done and you are safe."

The edge in his voice was palatable. She'd try to obey this command. She let her limbs relax, crushed her cheek against his shoulder. "How is Vicar Wilson?"

"The honorable man is down the hall. His daughter and Mrs. Tomàs are tending to him. He lost a lot of blood but he's going to live."

"Samuel will be well." A little part of her heart lifted.

A half-smirk filled Barrington's face. "Yes, he'll be able to flitter about you making me insanely jealous in no time."

"Mama's fine too? The duchess?"

He nodded and took her fingers to his lips. "Yes, both are. And, I'm grateful my mother-in-law is a great shot. How many son-in-laws can say that?" He sighed. "She ended this madness. James saw her aiming a flintlock through the window."

The safety of Barrington's arms couldn't stop Amora's trembles. Her insides churned. He was being so kind, but his heart must be broken with this baby gone. "What do we do now?"

He massaged her temples. "I'll have to go with Mrs. Tomàs to the magistrate's tomorrow, but under the circumstances... No charges should be made."

"Don't avoid the obvious. When do we grieve? How do we do this together? We can't lose us too."

Linking his palm with hers, he swept the union beneath the pillow to lie flat against her stomach. The weight of his heavy hand pressed her tiny one firmly against the soft chemise covering her middle. Fullness and a light flutter greeted her fingers. "You babble when you're tired."

Then the low, loving tones of his voice encircled her. "We still have a chance at this babe. Maybe it is a girl in your tummy with a stubbornness to live like her mother."

"Could be a boy with a hard head like his father."

"Perhaps." He kissed her forehead. "After your laying in, we'll move back to Tomàs Manor. I'm going to open grandfather's lands and do something to the Priory. I want all your nightmares gone."

With a soft kiss to the nape of her neck above the bandage, he glided his hands down her ribs, settling them on her abdomen. "Hudson and your mother with her herbs got you settled. Some rank mix of bark and laudanum, but your contractions weren't as bad as before. The blood loss was the problem. You've gotten stronger. Our love's been made stronger. God has not forgotten us."

This time joy flowed from her eyes. She closed them, not wanting a happy droplet to spill. "Thank you, God, for taking my shame."

"No, Amora. The shame is on the Charletons and Cynthia Miller for allowing this nightmare to continue."

She covered his hand. "We should tell Sarah. The news will be good for her."

"I've sent James with notes to Mr. Calloway and the Tantlins. All of England should rejoice that the Dark Walk Abductor is no more, but his victims should know first."

He swiped at his eyes and tossed his spectacles to the bed table. "Amora, I love you so much."

"I love you, too." She pulled at his powerful arms wanting him to enfold her within them as snuggly as possible. A smile filled her lungs, bubbling onto her lips. God had restored their marriage.

He nuzzled the edge of her brow. The soft whiskers from his unshaved chin tickled. "Thank God, for unveiling our love of all the secrets."

Epilogue

8 October, 1820, Clanville, England, Four months later

The sun started its rise into the sky. Leaving before daybreak from Winchester was the right idea for Barrington. He sat back in his seat as the carriage sailed over the last bend. He tapped his knee and tried to stop fidgeting. It seemed like an eternity being away from Tomàs Manor.

Would he catch Amora painting? Did she miss him as much as he missed her? His heart ached at the thought of not seeing any of her smiles. Even if his friend needed him, it wasn't enough to erase the pain of separating from his family. Everything he ever wanted was minutes away. God's greatest gift to man was a family's love.

"N-norton, you don't look v-victorious." Gerald Miller reached over and tugged Barrington's sleeve. "You still have a perfect record."

"Yes, I do." Barrington folded his arms, stilling his hands. "A perfect record of missing my wife, every day, every hour."

He glimpsed at his best friend. The man was a little thinner, but he had all his faculties. And now he was free, cleared of all charges.

"Miller, what will you do now? The tally of crimes has been wiped from your name. Will you join your sister in London?" The woman needed a chaperone of good character helping her.

"I don't know. It's a w-wide w-world out there. I've missed enough of it. Maybe I'll go with Cynthia on a tour of Europe. The world hasn't heard her voice."

Barrington nodded. Only Gerald's goodness could lead the witch back to a path of righteousness. Well, miracles did happen. "Well, if you run into trouble in London, my cousin Hudson will help you. I think he will settle there for a little while."

Miller nodded, but Barrington knew the man had to stretch his wings. "The offer to be my steward still stands. I'm going to need someone I trust to help me oversee Tomàs Orchards."

"I still can't picture you as a g-gentleman f-farmer."

With a tug on his tailcoat and a dip of his hat, Barrington smirked. "You'd be surprised at what the love of a good woman can do."

The rumble of the horse hooves finally quieted as the carriage stopped at the bottom of the path. Barrington didn't wait for James and leapt out the door.

He pivoted to Gerald. "You may have to stay the night. I've got something to attend to with James."

His friend nodded and held out a hand. "Thanks again, Norton. For everything."

"The offer still stands. When you have the wanderlust out of your system, be my steward. I need good friends. Go on and walk my grandfather's land and the vastness of the Tomàs orchards. You'll see that there is room for you here."

"We'll see. Got to make sure Cynthia's settled. She's given up her child long ago and now, her misguided love for you. She has nothing left but her voice and me." The rail thin man started humming and walked toward the apple trees.

James pulled Barrington's bag out of the back basket of the landau. "Here you go, sir. It will only take me a minute to change the horses. Where's Mr. Miller going? I thought he was heading back to London."

"Your work is done today." Barrington reached into his pocket and offered his man a folded letter. "This is for you."

The wind picked up, fluttering the parchment with his fingers. The thing almost caught flight, but Barrington clamped it down underneath his thumb.

With widened brown eyes, James reached for it. But, he wouldn't take the paper. "The wax crest. It's the Navy's. What is this?"

Barrington pointed his boot into a patch of thick grass and pressed down the blades. How to tell his loyal friend the worst?

James stood up straight, tugged on his deep blue livery. "Out with it, sir. The best medicine is a swift kick."

"The Admiralty responded to my inquiry about your son. The young man fought bravely in the battle of New Orleans, but his ship sunk for damages. He died saving a fellow landsman, another man impressed in to service with him."

Slowly, James took the paper and rolled it within his palms. "I thought as much..." His deep voice softened to whispers. "He didn't come back when the wars ended."

Barrington bowed his head. "Know he was a hero. Maybe there is comfort in that."

A deep swallow shook the set of James's strong jaw. "It's good to know. Thank you, sir. You solved one *no* for me."

His man turned back and started to climb atop the carriage. "James, don't return to work. Go, end your day."

James swiped at his eye. "No. The rushing air will do me good." His head lowered.

Barrington clasped his shoulder. "Not this time. Go head over to your quarters. Work will be here tomorrow. That's an order, my good man."

"Yes, sir." His man trudged up the hill and disappeared into Tomàs Manor.

A long sigh left Barrington. The news should have been better for such an excellent man. Family was a miracle. Head shaking, he climbed up and took the reins from the footman. The sooner the landau was stowed in the carriage house, the sooner Barrington could enjoy his blessings.

Stretching, Barrington bounced up the portico of Tomàs Manor. The vicar's dark boots balanced on the snowy rail.

"Morning, Mr. Norton." Wilson waved. "Good to have you back."

Leaning against a whitewashed post, Barrington shook his head. "I know I owe you, but don't you think it's about time you found a wife of your own so we can stop sharing?"

"I'm quite satisfied with God's groupings." With a handkerchief, Wilson brushed at the crumbs filling his face. "How did things go with Miller?"

"He's been freed. The prosecution merely read the charges as a formality. Charleton testified to his brother's guilt."

A sigh left the vicar's mouth. "Wonderful." The fellow smiled even as he leaned back into his chair. "I can breathe easier with the abductor's threats no longer dangling over our family."

"Our?" Barrington pulled off his gloves.

"I think my cousin knew. To know or suspect evil and do nothing is the worst. Playfair should've done better."

Barrington shrugged. "It's over, no time to condemn or convict the dead. Too much living to do."

Wilson brushed at a final crumb, one caught in the crease of his mouth. "Your workmen have broken open the Priory. Light now spills in every chamber."

Whipping off his top hat, Barrington stood up straight. "Good. Maybe it's time for Amora to visit it."

A frown leapt to the vicar's face as he stretched in the caned chair. "Are you sure?"

His heart didn't fear the feisty woman losing strength, not any more. "If she thinks she's ready, I will support her."

Mrs. Tomàs opened the door and brought a service of hot coffee out to the portico. "Oh, Samuel! My daughter, Regina, responded. We might be able to make amends too. I hope she allows a visit with her and her son in the spring." She swiped her eyes. "Oh, Mr. Norton. You've returned early."

"Can't bear to be away, ma'am." Barrington whipped off his hat and stuffed his gloves inside. "Where are they?"

"Neither, the baby nor Amora has awakened. I'll go--"

"No, Mrs. Tomàs." He stepped close and kissed her cheek. "Allow me."

The quiet of the house disappeared as a tiny cry met his ears. Hastening, he climbed the stairs and marched into the nursery. "There, there, Tomàs." He swaddled the boy and snuggled him in his arms. "Your proud Papa is here."

With dark blue eyes peering at Barrington, the babe suckled a bone button on his waistcoat. Sweet lilac wafted from the tuft of raven hair glued to the boy's head.

Barrington tickled the babe's face. "Have you missed me?"

The child suckled his thumb, but his soft cries started again.

"Let's go to your mother. She won't let a wet-nurse near you, so she has to make your tummy full."

On tiptoes, he plodded down the hall and eased into Amora's room. Her mural now stretched everywhere. The final section showed a woman smiling, holding a baby in her arms and a little one toddling by her hem. A man in spectacles gave chase. So life-like, so loving.

Wait. Another baby. He released a full sigh from his nostrils. It was just paint. Happy, wondrous paint. Oh, to imagine the colors. He was thankful for what he had, but if the Lord blessed...

Tomàs wiggled his arms and yanked on Barrington's cravat.

"Let's wake your mother with kisses." He cooed at Tomàs. "Come on, son."

He moved to the bed, pulled back the sheer curtains.

The mattress lay empty.

His heart crashed into his chest. Amora wasn't there.

Was she out walking? He hadn't seen her when he talked with James.

Puzzled, he edged to the window. "Let's see if Mama has slipped away to the orchards." Upon reaching the other side of the poster bed, he found his wife. She lay curled on the floor. A lone candle by her head.

His heart went to his throat. Would she be ever haunted?

He stroked his son's chin. Thank goodness the Lord gave Amora the daily strength to manage.

And He gave Barrington patience. For he needed it to keep Amora focused on their future.

Balancing the child in one hand, he leaned down and doused the flame. "Amora."

Kneeling beside his wife, he offered a light stroke to her cheek. That brought life to her violet eyes.

She sat up and craned her neck back and forth. "You're home. I'm so glad."

Tomàs wiggled as if to drop into her arms. Reaching, his little hand fisted around one of her curls.

"Yes, you know I can't bear even a minute apart from you two." He kissed her cold brow.

Her cheeks darkened as she pulled at her snowy chemise. Her breath quickened. "I shouldn't be on the floor. I don't know why--"

"Be at ease." He leaned in close and stole a short, sweet kiss. "I love your new paintings. Was I gone just two weeks?"

Prying open her son's chubby digits, she freed her tendril. "You've freed Mr. Miller?"

"Yes." Barrington scooped her up to the mattress and lowered Tomàs to her bosom. The sight of their son's brown face and dark hair against her tan skin made his chest feel full.

Barrington took off his spectacles and rested them on the bed table. A pile of his little notes lay tucked under the candle stand near her Bible. She read both every day.

Home, with his family intact, nothing could be better. A sigh of contentment seeped from his lungs. "Gerald Miller is now able to regain his life. He can choose what he wants to do with his years."

"Good, he's as much a victim as me and the other women." Her violet eyes widened as her kissable lips creased. "Are you sure you want this for yours? No more law books. A wife with challenges."

The bitter sweetness swirling in his gut at arguing his final case had disappeared. The minute Amora looked at him with all her love filling her eyes, any regret fled his skull. "I am home. I'm ready to spend my years with the best woman, managing these orchards and bringing hope to others that struggle. Take care of this hungry boy, then get dressed. It's time to go see the Priory. Do you still want too?"

She snuggled Tomàs. "Yes."

Amora inhaled the scent of the freshly cut pine. It made the air seem festive. She gripped Barrington's hand as he lifted her from the carriage, swinging her feet in the air.

The Priory seemed so different from the one she painted years ago, or the one she'd crawled away from on hands and knees.

Barrington pulled her close. His folded arms surrounded her head and straw bonnet. "I had the workmen tear away everything that blocked the light. No one will ever think they can hide in the Priory."

A hundred thoughts filled her head as they walked toward the ruins. Memories of screams echoed in her skull, but it didn't grip her heart. Barrington was with her. Light fell upon their linked gloves. God was also with them now, as he had been through all the pain.

"Do you want to see the cellar? We can see every bit of the small space."

She marched forward between stone pillars where a gate once stood. She fingered the blocks and traced the mortar and the edges of the missing ones. Her gaze fell upon the loose bricks scattered in the grass.

With all the sunlight heating the air, she shouldn't shiver. The Dark Walk Abductor was dead. His villainy could never happen again.

Nevertheless, she trembled.

"In your cellar, the workmen found a paint brush and this just outside." He put a small gold ring in her hand. The markings inside read, *Amora*.

Her strength began to wane. She leaned into Barrington. She was daft ever to think she could face this place without him.

"You're safe. You're free. And, you're beautiful." His low voice danced in her ear as the wool of his greatcoat blanketed her. She was truly safe and free, far from the young woman angry at God for taking her father or humbled by an abduction.

And beautiful, not just because Barrington loved her. She'd learned to love herself.

He kissed her brow and tightened his hold. "You don't have to go any farther. You are the bravest girl in the world."

"Maybe when Sarah arrives. Maybe we'll all go together." She swallowed the joyful sob gathering in her throat. "We'll make a merry party of it."

"Mr. Calloway agreed?"

"Yes, I wrote him of your plans to open a private asylum for victims of abduction. He wants her to have a normal life, too. Well, as normal as it can be."

He smoothed a curl behind her ear. "Who wants normal? Not me. I want every hour of everyday with you and a house full of extended family. Besides, someone needs to look after those who don't have a voice. I thought that's why I was called to the law. I know now I can use my inheritance and my blood to make a difference aiding victims, ensuring they don't feel invisible or broken. The Sanctuary built upon Norton land will do that."

"But the Old Bailey and London?"

He kissed her long and deep. "Not what I want."

She looped her arms about his neck and spun. The Priory now behind her.

"There will always be another barrister. Someone more eloquent with an easier temperament. But he's made only one man to be a father to Tomàs and a proper husband to you." He pulled back and crossed his arms. "Well, there is the reverend."

She shook her head. A full smile lifted her lips. "You're the only one for me. Your faithfulness and understanding saves me every day."

"Let's go visit Norton Hall." He claimed her arm and plodded toward the carriage. "I've had a few things tidied up. The workmen have splashed color on the walls."

With a hand to her hip, she spied his sheepish grin. "You chose more paints without me?"

"You are always at the top of mind, sweetheart." The

slow even tempo of his words contrasted with the sparks blazing within his gray eyes. Like melted silver fresh from an artisan's fire, his gaze engulfed her heart. "I tried to recreate the Mayfair attic in a wide upper loft space, but I need your thoughts on improvements."

"More pillows?" She hiked up her hem and ran to the carriage. Her short boot heels made easy work of the land she so loved. "What are we waiting for? You've been gone a fortnight. I know how you get when we've been separated for one day. "

He caught up with her, clasped her hand, and brushed his lips gently against her wrist. "You are my love, Amora. I see all of you, every bit. I couldn't love or admire you more."

She knew in her heart this was true. They finally saw the truth of each other without filters or blinders. The magnificent work that God had started within them had been made complete. Together they held enough strength, peace, and unity to last forever, even through future storms.

The End

Please Leave A Review

If you like these stories, please leave a review.

I love being able to write these books. I hope you love them too. As an author, I depend on you, the reader, to get the word out about my books. If you liked this book, please leave a review online and recommend it to a friend. The more you spread the word, the more books I can write and nothing would please me more than to create more of these stories for you.

Thank you.

Vanessa Riley

Extras

Author's Note

Dear Friend,

I enjoyed writing Unveiled Love because diverse Regency London needs its story told, and I am a sucker for a wonderful husband and wife romance. They need love after the vows, too.

These stories will showcase a world of intrigue and romance, a setting everyone can hopefully find a character to identify with in the battle of love, which renews and gives life.

Stay in touch. Sign up at www.vanessariley.com for my newsletter. You'll be the first to know about upcoming releases, and maybe even win a sneak peek.

Thank so much for giving this book a read.

Vanessa Riley

Many of my readers are new to Regencies, so I always

add notes and a glossary to make items readily available. If you know of a term that should be added to enhance my readers' knowledge, send them to me at: vanessa@christianregency.com. I will acknowledge you in my next book.

Here are my notes:

Mulatto Barristers

I couldn't find definitive proof of one, but that does not mean it was impossible. Connections and success bent rules. Such was the case for William Garrow (1760-1840). He was not born a gentleman and didn't go to the best schools. Yet, his success in the courts rewrote how trials would be performed. He introduced the premise, "presumed innocent until proven guilty," and rose to become Solicitor General for England and Wales.

Free blacks in 1800's English Society

By Regency times, historians, Kirstin Olsen and Gretchen Holbrook Gerzina, estimate that Black London (the black neighborhood of London) had over 10,000 residents. While England led the world in granting rights to the enslaved and ending legal slavery thirty years before the American Civil War, it still had many citizens who were against change. Here is another image from an anti-abolitionist.

The New Union Club being a representation of what took place at a celebrated dinner given by a celebrated society – includes in picture abolitionists, Billy Waters, Zachariah Macauley, William Wilberforce. – published 19 July 1819. Source: Wiki Commons

Notable People Mentioned in this Serial

William Wilberforce (1759-1833) was an abolitionist who sought to end England's slave trade which existed within the Empire's colonies. His conversion to Evangelical Christianity made him change his outlook on life and to seek reform.

Zachary Macaulay (1768-1838) was an abolitionist and a former governor of Sierra Leone. Like Wilberforce, his faith drove him to try to end the slave trade.

George Bridgetower (George Augustus Polgreen Bridgetower) was born in Poland on October 11, 1778. The mulatto described as Afro-European was the son of John Frederick Bridgetower, a West Indie's black man and a white German maid. He became a virtuoso violinist whose talents were recognized by the Prince Regent. The prince took an interest in his education and directed Bridgetower's musical studies. Bridgetower performed in many concerts in London theatres like, Covent Garden, Drury Lane and the Haymarket Theatre. In the spring of 1789, Bridgetower performed at the Abbaye de Panthemont in Paris. Thomas Jefferson attended this event. Bridgewater died February 1860.

Harriet Westbrook was the first wife of Percy Shelley. She was abandoned by Lord Shelley when he fell in love with **Mary Wollstonecraft.** On 10 December 1816, Harriet's body was found. She was pregnant when she was drowned in the the Serpentine in Hyde Park, London.

King George III, the king who lost the American colonies, suffered from bouts of mental illness. His son ruled in his stead as the Prince Regent (George Augustus Frederick). King George III died January 27, 1820. Mourning for a King had three parts: deep mourning (eight weeks), mourning (two weeks), and half-mourning (two weeks). During these times, clothing and accessories had to be correlated to the type of mourning.

The NEW UNION-CLUB

Inter-racial marriages occurred.

The children known as mulattos lived lives on the scale of their education and wealth. Examine this painting. Portrait of a Mulatto by FABRE, François-Xavier. It is from 1809-1810. Portraits were indicative to status and wealth. My screenshot of the image the art once displayed at Arenski Fine Art, LTD London. More information can be found at http://

Vanessa Riley

maryrobinettekowal.com/journal/images-of-regency-era-free-people-of-colour/.

This painting of an interracial couple and child, *Pintura de Castas*, from Spaniard and Mulatto, Morisca

(1763). Where love exists barriers fade.

Slavery in England

The emancipation of slaves in England preceded America by thirty years and freedom was won by legal court cases not bullets.

Somerset v Stewart (1772) is a famous case, which established the precedence for the rights of slaves in England. The English Court of King's Bench, led by Lord Mansfield, decided that slavery was unsupported by the common law of England and Wales. His ruling:

"The state of slavery is of such a nature that it is incapable of being introduced on any reasons, moral or political, but only by positive law, which preserves its force long after the reasons, occasions, and time itself from whence it was created, is erased from memory. It is so odious, that nothing can be suffered to support it, but positive law. Whatever inconveniences, therefore, may follow from the decision, I cannot say this case is allowed or approved by the law of England; and therefore the black must be discharged."

E. Neville William, The Eighteenth-Century Constitution: 1688-1815, pp: 387-388.

The Slavery Abolition Act 1833 was an act of Parliament, which abolished slavery throughout the British Empire. A fund of $20 Million Pound Sterling was set up to compensate slave owners. Many of the highest society families were compensated for losing their slaves.

This act did exempt the territories in the possession of the East India Company, the Island of Ceylon, and the Island of Saint Helena. In 1843, the exceptions were eliminated.

Glossary

The Regency – The Regency is a period of history from 1811-1825 (sometimes expanded to 1795-1837) in England. It takes its name from the Prince Regent who ruled in his father's stead when the king suffered mental illness. The Regency is known for manners, architecture, and elegance. Jane Austen wrote her famous novel, *Pride and Prejudice* (1813), about characters living during the Regency.

England is a country in Europe. London is the capital city of England.

Image of England from a copper engraved map created by William Darton in 1810.

Port Elizabeth was a town founded in 1820 at the tip of South Africa. The British settlement was an attempt to strengthen England's hold on the Cape Colony and to be a buffer from the Xhosa.

Xhosa - A proud warrior people driven to defend their land and cattle-herding way of life from settlers expanding the boundaries of the Cape Colony.

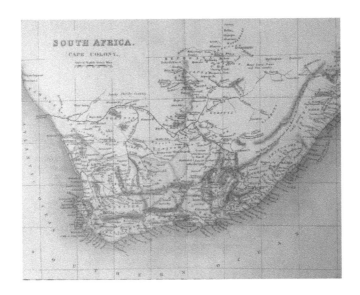

Image of South Africa from a copper engraved map created by John Dower in 1835.

Abigail – A lady's maid.

Soiree – An evening party.

Bacon-brained – A term meaning foolish or stupid.

Black – A description of a black person or an African.

Black Harriot – A famous prostitute stolen from Africa, then brought to England by a Jamaican planter who died, leaving her without means. She turned to harlotry to earn a living. Many members of the House of Lords became her clients. She is described as tall, genteel, and alluring, with a degree of politeness.

Blackamoor – A dark-skinned person.

Bombazine – Fabric of twilled or corded cloth made of silk and wool or cotton and wool. Usually the material was dyed black and used to create mourning clothes.

Breeched – The custom of a young boy no longer wearing pinafores and now donning breeches. This occurs about age six.

Breeches – Short, close-fitting pants for men, which fastened just below the knees and were worn with stockings.

Caning – A beating typically on the buttocks for naughty behavior.

Compromise – To compromise a reputation is to ruin or cast aspersions on someone's character by catching them with the wrong people, being alone with someone who wasn't a relative at night, or being caught doing something wrong. During the Regency, gentlemen were often forced to marry women they had compromised.

Dray – Wagon.

Footpads – Thieves or muggers in the streets of London.

Greatcoat – A big outdoor overcoat for men.

Mews – A row of stables in London for keeping horses.

Pelisse - An outdoor coat for women that is worn over a dress.

Quizzing Glass – An optical device, similar to a monocle, typically worn on a chain. The wearer might use the quizzing glass to look down upon people.

Reticule – A cloth purse made like a bag that had a drawstring closure.

Season – One of the largest social periods for high society in London. During this time, a lady attended a variety of balls and soirees to meet potential mates.

Sideboard – A low piece of furniture the height of a writing desk, which housed spirits.

Ton – Pronounced *tone*, the *ton* was a high class in society during the Regency era.

Sneak Peak: Unmasked Heart

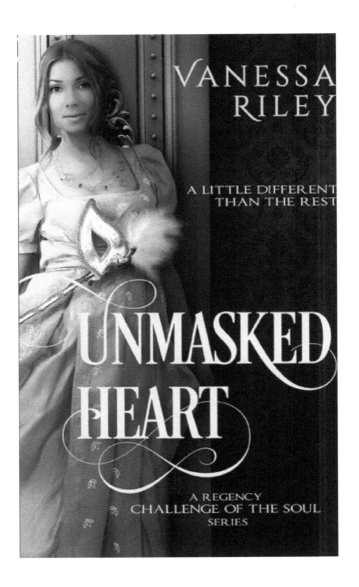

VANESSA
RILEY

A LITTLE DIFFERENT
THAN THE REST

UNMASKED
HEART

A REGENCY
CHALLENGE OF THE SOUL
SERIES

Shy, nearsighted caregiver, Gaia Telfair always wondered why her father treated her a little differently than her siblings, but she never guessed she couldn't claim his love because of a family secret, her illicit birth. With everything she knows to be true evaporating before her spectacles, can the mulatto passing for white survive being exposed and shunned by the powerful duke who has taken an interest in her?

Ex-warrior, William St. Landon, the Duke of Cheshire, will do anything to protect his mute daughter from his late wife's scandals. With a blackmailer at large, hiding in a small village near the cliffs of Devonshire seems the best option, particularly since he can gain help from the talented Miss Telfair, who has the ability to help children learn to speak. If only he could do a better job at shielding his heart from the young lady, whose honest hazel eyes see through his jests as her tender lips challenge his desire to remain a single man.

Unmasked Heart is the first Challenge of the Soul Regency novel.

Excerpt from Unmasked Heart: The Wrong Kiss

Seren adjusted the delicate gauzy silk flowers lining the edges of Gaia's cape. "Wait here until your Elliot arrives. Don't leave this room; I'll come back to find you."

Part of Gaia didn't want to release Seren's hand. Half-seeing things made the room frightening. Her pulse raced. "What if someone else arrives?"

"Tell them the room is occupied. They'll understand." Seren adjusted her silvery sarsenet cape, balanced the scales she hung on a cord in place of a reticule, and smoothed her wide skirts.

Grasping hold of the armrest, Gaia forced her lips to smile. "Good luck to you, Lady Justice. I hope you have fun."

"If you find the love you seek, I'll be happy. You deserve happiness for being you, not someone's daughter. Tell Elliot of your love. Gaia, you need a name and a household of your own, where secrets can't harm you." She gave Gaia a hug. "I want your cup filled with joy."

"Even if my cup isn't pure."

"Your heart is untainted by the past, made pure by salvation. That's what matters." Seren put a hand to Gaia's face. In the candlelight, she and Seren, their skin, looked the same. "Live free tonight."

Seren moved out of focus and left the room, closing the door behind her.

The lime blur of the settee was as comfortable as it was big, but Gaia couldn't sit still. She fidgeted and tapped her slippers on the floor. The ticking of the mantle clock filled the quiet room.

Trying to ignore it, she clutched the ribbons of her papier-mâché mask and straightened its creamy feathers. She stood and, with the pace of a turtle, she moved to the fireplace and strained to see where the limbs of timepiece pointed. Nine-fifteen.

Elliot would be here soon. What would she say to him? Would she remain silent and just dance with him?

She leveled her shoulders. How could she not say her peace, as she looked into his blue eyes? How ironic to unmask her heart at a masquerade ball.

The moon finally broke through the clouds and cast its light into the salon. Whether from the fuzziness of her vision or the beauty of the glow, the window glass sparkled, as did the mirrors and polished candleholders of the small room.

The low tones of the musicians started up again. The jaunty steps of a reel sounded. The tone called to her feet again, and she danced as if she were in someone's arms. The beechnut- colored walls and white moldings swirled as she did.

That set ended and then another and another. She paced in front of the mantle clock. It tolled a low moan as it struck ten. Elliot had missed their appointment. Heaviness weighed upon Gaia, from the crown of her costume's veils to the thick folds of her opal domino.

How ironic to stand in such finery, when Mr. Telfair told her she wasn't worthy. Yet hadn't she schemed with her stepmother and Seren to be here? Gaia should leave. Too many wrongs would never equal righteousness.

Movement outside the room sent her pulse racing. Maybe Elliot had been detained, but was still coming. She wrung her hands and looked to the shining circle on the door, its crystal knob.

The footsteps passed by, the sound diminishing, as did her dreams.

Elliot wouldn't show. He must still think of her as a child, as Julia's hapless sister, as Millicent's plain cousin. Or maybe Julia had told him. They could be laughing about it now.

Sighs and a misguided tear leaked out. She leaned against the burnished mantle. The warmth of the hearth did nothing to thaw her suddenly-cold feet. It was best he didn't show. He'd saved her the embarrassment of his rejection. A mulatto's dance or kiss could never do for him.

The rhythm of a dance set crept beneath the ivory doorframe. Maybe Elliot found a new young lady, whose large dowry like Millicent's made her irresistible to men. Was she in his arms, basking in the glow of his smile, his fun conversation?

The ache in her bosom swelled. Gaia released her breath, stilling her trembling fingers against the sheer veil of her fairy costume. Perhaps she should slip from the room and run into the moonlight of the moors.

The door opened. The strains of violin-play seeped into the salon.

Elliot in his domino cape and ebony half-mask entered the room. "Excuse me," his voice was low, hoarse. He whipped a handkerchief from his pocket and wiped his mouth as he bowed.

Always so formal, but what a pity his melodious voice sounded raspy.

Now or never. She cleared her throat and, in her most sultry manner, she placed her hands to her hips and curtsied. "I've been waiting for you."

"Excuse me, do I know you?" He tugged at the ribbons of his mask.

Waving her arms, she caught his gaze. "Please don't take it off. I won't be able to get through this if you expose your handsome face."

"I see." He stopped, his strong hands lowering beneath the cape of his domino. "Miss Telfair?"

With a quick motion, she whipped up her airy silk skirts and traipsed closer, but maintained an easy distance on the other side of the settee. "Call me Gaia.

We needn't be so formal."

His head moved from side-to-side, as if to scan the room.

"You needn't fret, sir. We are quite alone. That's why I decided to confess my feelings."

"I see."

Must he continue to act as if he didn't know her? The moonbeams streaming through the thick window mullions surrounded him, and reflected in the shiny black silk of his cape. Could he be taller, more intimidating?

Elliot had to think of her as a woman. She straightened her shoulders. "I'm so glad you've come. I know I'm young, but not too young to know my heart."

"Miss Telfair, I think this is some sort of mistake."

Blood pounding in her ears, she swept past the settee and stood within six feet of him. "Please call me Gaia."

"I'll not trespass on your privacy any longer." He spun, as if to flee.

She shortened the distance and caught his shoulder. "Please don't go. It took a lot to garner the courage to meet you here."

With a hesitance she'd never seen from confident Elliot, he gripped her palm and kissed her satin glove. "I know it takes a great amount of courage to make a fool of one's self."

"There's no better fool than one in love." She slipped his hand to her cheek. "Why hide behind mocking? I know you. I've seen your heart. The way you take care of that precious little girl as if she were your own." It touched Gaia, witnessing Elliot helping his brother's household as if it were his own.

"How did you know my fear?" He drew his hand to

163

his mouth. "You see too much."

Squinting, he still wasn't quite in focus. He shifted his weight and rubbed his neck, as if her compliments made him nervous.

"This is a mistake. We should forget this conversation. A man shouldn't be alone with such a forthright young lady. I will return to the ball." He leveled his broad shoulders and marched to the door, his heels clicking the short distance.

Maybe being so low was freeing. "Why leave?" she let her voice sound clear, no longer cautioned with shyness or regret. "Here can be no worse than out there, with the other ladies readying to weigh your pockets."

His feet didn't move, but he closed the door, slamming it hard. Had she struck a nerve?

He pivoted to face her. "Aren't you just like them, my dear? Weren't all gentle women instructed to follow a man's purse? No? Perhaps torturing is your suit, demanding more and more until nothing remains of his soul."

"Men hunt for dowries, and they know best how to torture someone; ignoring people who want their best; separating friends, even sisters, in their pursuits. The man who raised me did so begrudgingly, just to make me a governess to my brother. Is there no worse torture than to yearn to be loved and no one care?"

"A governess? I think I understand."

This wasn't how she'd expected this conversation to go. Elliot's graveled words possessed an edge as sharp as a sword. He seemed different, both strong and vulnerable. It must be the costumes, freeing them both from the confining roles they lived.

Yet he didn't move. He didn't feel the same.

She fanned her shimmering veil. Half-seeing and disguised, she could be as bold and as direct as Millicent or Seren. Gaia could even face the truth. "I forgive you for not feeling the same."

She'd said it, and didn't crumble when he didn't respond in kind. Maybe this was best. With the release of a pent-up breath, she added, "I wish you well."

He chuckled, the notes sounding odd for Elliot's laugh. "Has a prayer wrought this transformation? Well, He works in mysterious ways."

Maybe it was all the prayers over the years that built up her strength. Amazing. Elliot didn't love her, and no tears came to her. Well, numbness had its benefit. "Good evening. You can go; my friend Seren will be back soon."

When he finally moved, it was to come closer, near enough she trail her pinkie along the edgings of his domino, but that, too, was a cliff she wasn't ready to jump.

"Gaia, what if I'm not ready to leave?"

Her ears warmed, throbbing with the possibilities of his meaning.

"If I am trapped," his voice dropped to a whisper, "it is by your hands."

Her heart clenched at his words. Elliot never seemed more powerful or more dangerous. "I'd hope I, ah, maybe I should be leaving."

He took a half-step, as if to block her path. His outline remained a blur; a tall, powerful blur. "You've had your say, sweet Gaia. Now it is my turn."

This near, she could smell the sweet starch of his thick cravat and a bit of spice. Her heart beat so loudly. Could he hear it?

He drew a thumb down her cheek. "Pretty lady, your

eyes are red. Your cheeks are swollen. What made you cry so hard? And why didn't you find me?"

Something was different about the tone of his hushed voice. There was pain in it. Did he hurt because Gaia had? Could she have discounted the possibility of Elliot returning affections too quickly?

Something dark and formidable drew her to him like never before. "How could I find you? I didn't know you cared, not until this moment."

His arms went about her, and he cradled her against his side. His fingers lighted in her bun. "I'm fascinated with the curl and color of your hair."

Too many thoughts pressed as a familiar tarragon scent tightened its grip about her heart. "Not course or common—"

His lips met her forehead. His hot breath made her shiver and lean more into him. "Never; that's what I've been trying to tell you."

Heady, and a little intoxicated by the feel of his palms on her waist, she released her mask. It fluttered to the floor. Its pole drummed then went silent on the wood floor. She dropped her lids and raised her chin. "I guess this is when you kiss me. Know the lips of someone who esteems you, not your means or connections."

"A lass as beautiful as you needn't ask or wait for a buffoon to find you alone in a library." His arm tightened about her, and he pulled her beneath his cape. The heat of him made her swoon, dipping her head against his broad chest. He tugged a strand of her curls, forcing her chignon to unravel and trail her back. "Now you look the part of a fairy, an all-knowing auburn-haired Gypsy."

He lifted her chin and pressed his mouth against her sealed lips. However, with less than a few seconds of rapture, he relented and released her shoulders.

She wrapped her arms about his neck and wouldn't release him. "I'm horrible. This is my first kiss. I'm sorry." She buried her face against his waistcoat.

His quickened breath warmed her cheek. "Then it should be memorable." His head dipped forward, with the point of his mask, the delicate paper nose, trailing her brows, nudging her face to his. Slowly drawing a finger across her lips, his smooth nail, the feel of his rough warm skin, made them vibrate, relax, then part. "Trust me, Gaia."

She wanted to nod her consent, but didn't dare move from his sensuous touch.

"Let a real kiss come from a man who covets your friendship, who thinks you are beautiful." He dropped his domino to the floor.

Read more of <u>Unmasked Heart</u> at VanessaRiley.com.

Sneak Peak: The Bargain III

Episode III of The Bargain
Length: 11 Chapters (30,000 words)
Summary: Secrets Revealed

Excerpt: The Aftermath of a Kiss and the Xhosa

"Captain," Ralston cleared his throat. "She fixed me up and a number of others."

The baron's lips pursed as he nodded. "Miss Jewell is full of surprises."

His hair was wild and loose. He smelled of beach sand and perspiration. Still frowning, he raised Ralston's arm a few inches from the boat's deck. "Looks like you will live."

"Don't know how much good that'll do me here, Captain. We left here with peace. Why? What happened? And Mr. Narvel?"

"I don't know, but I'm going to find the answers." Using Mr. Ralston's good arm, the captain pulled him to stand. "Get yourself below and sleep. I've got men on watch. Our guns are ready this time for any other surprises."

The sailor shrugged as he tested his shoulder, pushing at the wrapped muscles. "Yes, Sir."

Lord Welling leaned down and took Precious's hand. "You've helped enough, Miss Jewell. I want you to go down below."

She shook her head. "There's more I can do up here."

The baron snatched her up by the elbow. "I insist."

Precious shook free and grabbed up the doctoring supplies. "We're probably going to need these again."

Ralston closed his eyes and grunted almost in unison

with Lord Welling before trudging past the other men laying out on the deck, the one's whose injured legs prevented them from going below. With no rain, they'd be alright under the night sky.

Precious looked up into the night sky that looked like black velvet with twinkling diamonds. Such innocence shrouds this place. So opposite the truth.

"Come along, Miss Jewel. Now." The baron's voice sounded of distant thunder, quiet and potent. His patience, his anger, at so many lost this night must be stirring. He again put his hands around her shoulders and swept her forward.

She didn't like to be turned so abruptly, but stopping in her tracks didn't seem right either. So she slowed her steps, dragging her slippers against the planks of the Margeaux. "What are you doing?"

He stopped and swung her around so that she faced him. "I need your help telling Mrs. Narvel. It's not going to be easy telling a pregnant woman that—"

"Her husband has died at the Xhosa's hands." Precious's heart drummed loudly, like a death gait. Staying busy helping the injured delayed the building grief she had for her friend. Oh, how was Clara to take it?

Lord Welling's lips thinned and pressed into a line. "It's never easy telling a woman a difficult truth or waiting for her to admit it."

She caught his gaze. It felt as if the fire within it scorched her. Suddenly, the smell of him, the closeness of his stance made her pulse race. He wasn't talking about Clara, but Precious wasn't ready to admit anything.

And what would he think if she told him that at that

moment with Xhosa bearing down upon them that nothing seemed more right than to dive headlong to save him. No, Lord Welling didn't need that bug in his ear.

But soon, he'd press. He wasn't the kind of man who waited for anything.

He gripped her hand and led her into the darkness where those stars twinkled in his eyes. "Precious, I need to ask you something."

Chin lifting, she pushed past him and headed for the hole and the ladder below. "We need to get to Mrs. Narvel."

She took her time climbing down, making sure of her footing on each rung, then she waited at the bottom for her employer, the man who in the middle of chaos kissed her more soundly than any one ever had.

His boots made a gentle thud as he jumped the last rungs. When he pivoted, he crowded her in the dark corner, towering over her. "You're reckless, Precious."

She backed up until she pressed against the compartment's planked wall. "I'm not the only one. Taking Jonas to a land of killing, that's reckless."

He clutched the wall above each of her shoulders, but he might as well had gripped them with his big hands. There was no escape from the truth he was waiting on.

Leaning within an inch of her, his voice reached a loud scolding tone. "You're reckless. Wanton for danger."

Her face grew warm and she bit down on her traitorous lips, ones that wanted a taste of him again.

His breathing seemed noisier. His hands moved to within inches of her arms, but they didn't sneak about her. No, those fingers stayed flat against the wood, tempting, teasing of comfort. "You could've been killed. Will you ever listen?"

The harshness of his tone riled up her spirit. "Won't do me no good to listen if you're dead. The least you can say is thank you."

He straightened and towed one hand to his neck. Out of habit, she squinted as if he'd strike her, but she knew in her bones that wasn't to happen. The fear of him hurting her was long gone. Only the fright of him acting again on that kiss between them remained. "What am I to do with you?"

Get the next Episode. Look for all the episodes. Join my newsletter to stay informed.

Join My Newsletter, Free Goodies

Thank you for taking the time to read Unveiling Love. If you enjoyed it, please consider telling your friends or posting a short review (Amazon or Goodreads). Word of mouth is an author's best friend and much appreciated. Thank you.

Also, sign up for my newsletter and get the latest news on this series or even a free book. I appreciate your support.

VR

Let me point you to some free books, just for reading this far:

Free Book: The Bargain - Episode I:

Coming to London has given Precious Jewell a taste of freedom, and she will do anything, bear anything, to keep it. Defying her master is at the top of her mind, and she won't let his unnerving charm sway her. Yet, will her restored courage lead her to forsake a debt owed to the grave and a child who is as dear to her as her own flesh?

Gareth Conroy, the third Baron Welling, can neither abandon his upcoming duty to lead the fledgling colony of Port Elizabeth, South Africa nor find the strength to be a good father to his heir. Every look at the boy reminds him of the loss of his wife. Guilt over her death plagues his sleep, particularly when he returns to London. Perhaps the spirit and fine eyes of her lady's maid, Precious Jewell, might offer the beleaguered baron a new reason to dream.

Free Book: A Taste of Traditional Regency Romances: Extended excerpts of Regency novels (Bluestocking League Book 1)

From some of the most beloved authors of Regency romance come stories to delight. These excerpts, set in the time of Jane Austen, will give you a sip of sweet romance and will leave you eager for more.

Gail Eastwood, The Captain's Dilemma: Escaped French war prisoner Alexandre Valmont has risked life and honor in a desperate bid to return home and clear his name. Merissa Pritchard risks charges of treason and her family's safety to help the wounded fugitive. But will they risk their hearts in a most dangerous game of love?

From Camille Elliot, The Spinster's Christmas:

Spinster Miranda Belmoore and naval Captain Gerard Foremont, old childhood friends, meet again for a large Christmas party at Wintrell Hall. Miranda is making plans to escape a life of drudgery as a poor relation in her cousin's household, while Gerard battles bitterness that his career was cut short by the injury to his knee. However, an enemy has infiltrated the family party, bent on revenge and determined that Twelfth Night will end in someone's death ...

April Kihlstrom, The Wicked Groom: When the Duke of Berenford is engaged to marry a woman he's never met, what's a poor man to do? How was he to know she wouldn't appreciate his brilliant scheme?

From Vanessa Riley, Unmasked Heart: Shy, nearsighted caregiver, Gaia Telfair never guessed she couldn't claim her father's love because of a family secret, her illicit birth. Can the mulatto passing for white survive being exposed and shunned by the powerful duke who has taken an interest in her? William St. Landon, the Duke of Cheshire, will do anything to protect his mute daughter from his late wife's scandals. He gains the help of Miss Telfair, who has the ability to help children learn to speak, but with a blackmailer at large, if only he could do a better job at shielding his heart.

Regina Scott, Secrets and Sensibilities: When art teacher Hannah Alexander accompanies her students on a country house visit, she never dreams of entering into a dalliance with the handsome new owner David Tenant. But one moment in his company and she's in danger of losing her heart, and soon her very life.